The Cold Case: a Vintage Murder

A sassy, smart and snotty cozy mystery

Christa Bakker

Counting Blessings

Contents

To Ariëlle and Raphaël, who wanted their name in a book

1

Cactus is trying to reach you

It was coming. I could feel it creeping up on me.

I was in my living room, having just sent home another happy client. She could now look forward to a bunch of sassy peekaboo pin-up photos, and I could look… deep into the glass of undiluted *pastis* in my hand. My one defence. My last hope.

Pastis, with the over 40 percent alcohol it contains, kills off the first signs of a stomach bug. That's common knowledge. But I wanted it to step out of its jurisdiction and kill the thing attacking my throat on its way to my stomach.

As I sat there, contemplating the yellow syrupy liquid, my young (and altogether too sexy for his own good) assistant Thibault ambled into the room, carrying my phone.

'What is it, Beau?' I asked as I put the glass to my lips.

'You have a message from someone called Cactus?'

I gasped. The alcohol shot into my windpipe. Pain! For several excruciating seconds, I could do nothing but endure the searing burn, coughing like a madwoman to get the biting liquid out of my lungs. Wheezing and with tears streaming over my cheeks, I looked up at Beau, who waited patiently for me to turn human again.

'There's a reason people put water in that, you know.' No concern whatsoever. Thanks, man.

'Sorry, what was that?' I croaked with watery eyes. I must have misheard his first statement. It couldn't be.

'I said Cactus is trying to reach you. Who's Cactus?'

After all these years. My insides turned to cream that was rapidly being whipped. With sugar. I'm talking butterflies on steroids. I gripped my stomach in an unsuccessful attempt to calm it.

My charming assistant must have thought I couldn't handle the *pastis*, but his dramatic eye-roll froze when I downed the rest of the drink in one gulp. Both his eyebrows shot up. 'Who *is* this guy?'

I took a deep breath, holding it for a few seconds to drain the air of as much courage as it would give me. 'I knew him. Years ago. When I was still married to your uncle.'

Beau frowned while he went through a list in his head. 'He's a friend of Franck's? I don't know any of them that go by Cactus. What's his real name?'

'Léon Levotre.' I sighed. 'But you wouldn't know him. He's not a criminal.' I reached for the bottle of *pastis* to see if I could get it to work on my throat this time, but Beau strode over and stopped me, concern in his eyes.

'Are you going to tell me, or am I going to have to google him?'

I grabbed the bottle from under his hand with a little prickle of annoyance, but then realised his worry was genuine. 'It's not what you think. He's not a threat. Not any more.'

Beau's frown deepened as he sat down on the couch next to me. 'That doesn't comfort me at all.'

'Look, this has nothing to do with you. He's just a guy. A great guy. Teaches economics. I met him a little more than a year after Franck and I got married, so just around the time Franck had scared off most of my friends and family. I needed someone, and Léon was... amazing. We had a few drinks, talked about everything and nothing, but... Well, you know...'

'Franck found out.' Beau's voice was hard. The kind of hardness he reserved just for my ex.

'No! Not even that. I don't think.' Suddenly I wasn't sure. At the time, I'd been elated to find a new friend. To know that it wasn't me who'd become incapable of being the kind of person other people wanted to be around. I never told Franck about Léon, but thinking back, he must have noticed a change in me. Did he find out? Was that the real reason why Léon eventually stopped texting?

I stared at my empty glass. 'Léon was a little too perfect. We'd been friends for a few months when I realised I was falling for him. And even though Franck had lost his attraction, we were still married. My guilt over my feelings played right into Franck's hand because I went along with his desire to keep me at home more. I made up excuses not to meet Léon for coffee. He seemed to understand, but we stayed in contact. Until we didn't. That was around the time I found out where Franck really got his money. I foolishly shared my findings with Léon, who by then had become my only friend, albeit a digital one. I think I got one more text after that. Something empty, like "that sucks" or something. And that was it. No more friends.'

I paused to sniffle. Hm, maybe the alcohol was already too late if I had sniffles in addition to a sore throat. 'But it didn't matter. That was in November before that last Christmas at your mum's.'

Thibault let my explanation sink in. 'So why call him Cactus?'

I pulled up a corner of my mouth, though it didn't feel like a smile. 'To remind myself not to get too close.'

But maybe *I* had been the cactus. In fact, I was pretty sure I was. That made it all the more curious, though, that he'd contact me now, over five years and a whole bunch of trouble later. I held up my hand.

'Let's see what he wants, shall we?'

Beau held on to my phone. '*T'es sûre?* If he didn't want anything to do with you when you were in trouble...'

I gave him a pointed look. 'May I remind you that I hadn't seen *you* in five years when you came knocking?'

The phone landed in my outstretched palm. Two swallows later, I pulled up the message, read it, and showed it to Beau.

Dear Julie, I'm coming to Saint-Maurice. Would love to see you. Léon.

'Looks like he knows where you are.'

I nodded.

Staring at my screen, he frowned. 'There's just one message.'

I hummed in acknowledgement and sighed. 'After the trial, I didn't keep anything that reminded me of Franck, including my phone. I lost more than just my message history in my hurry to get rid of Franck's influence, but at the time, I didn't care.'

'So what are you going to tell this Cactus? Do you want to see him?'

My heart silently said yes. My head said out loud, 'I don't know.'

Beau got up. 'Well, if you don't, I'd be happy to tell him so for you. Just let me know.'

That brought a real smile to my face. I didn't need his protection. Especially not against Léon. But it was sweet of him to offer. As Beau retreated to the kitchen, I finally filled my glass again. If it didn't help fight the bug in my throat, it might give me wisdom about what to do.

An hour later, I was still on the couch with the now empty glass in my hand. Memories going round and round in my head had made me fill up the glass once too many times, and my former friend had become both a hero and a villain in my thoughts. A hero for saving my sanity when I thought the only person who could still bear to be around me was a husband who didn't like me any more. A villain for abandoning me at the worst moment and leaving me with a criminal in an abusive relationship. After an hour, I still didn't know which to pick.

My life with Franck had been a constant struggle – first to keep him happy when he seemed so disappointed in me, and later to keep him calm and convince him that I was still doing what he told me to do 'for my own good'. Keeping my friendship with Léon secret had only added to the mental pressure. So much so that I'd wanted to give up on it more than once, but giving up on that one friendship would have been like giving up on life.

When I finally broke free – when Franck was in jail rather than in the next room – Léon had been on my mind more than ever. But with the freedom also came an unexpected insecurity. Had he been genuine, or had I been his good deed for the day?

Maybe Franck hadn't been entirely wrong about me, and my one friend was not a true friend after all. When he stopped messaging, my suspicions were confirmed. But looking back now, it didn't make sense that Léon would spend years keeping in contact only to drop off the radar when my situation changed for the better. Was he a hero, or was he a villain?

Thibault came in from the courtyard, surprised to see me where he left me. '*Bon, ça suffit.* Let's head to Jeanette's for an *apéro*. Or a *tisane*, in your case. Undiluted *pastis*...' He muttered the last bit with a shake of his head, like he was my mother.

I rose unsteadily, for once not minding that he took charge. The walk into the village would do me good, as would the sight of the café owner. Jeanette Ta had been my instant friend when I returned to Saint-Maurice, but now that I'd invested in her dream of fixing up the old hotel, she'd become my business partner as well. Every time I saw her, she had some sort of update for me, delivered with the same gusto whether it was good or bad news. It'd be good to have the distraction.

I grabbed my coat and purse and left the house, leaning heavily on Beau's arm. I hadn't had enough alcohol to throw me off balance, but his presence was reassuring. After my hour mentally spent in the past, I liked being physically reminded that in the present, I had friends again. People to literally lean on

I took a deep breath and put my thumb and forefinger to my temple. Collecting all my insecurities and anxiety at that one point, I pulled them from my brain. Thibault had seen me do this a million times before and had run out of jokes about it, but even he would realise that this was not the time. My silly little exercise worked. I shook the imaginary dark rag now clinging to my fingers off at the side of the road, resisting the urge to dig a hole and bury it.

By the time we reached the café, shocked out of my slump by the crisp January air, I'd come to a conclusion. My life was different now. *I* was different now. I was more confident. And, most importantly, I was not alone. If Léon found a reason to abandon me again, I wouldn't fall into a void. I would fall into the outstretched arms of my friends. No, strike that. I wouldn't fall at all!

I'd let Léon know that I'd be ready for him.

Of course, after sending that message to Léon, I spent the rest of the evening disguising the fact that I felt extremely unready. Whenever I thought I'd successfully let go of the past, my shoulders tensed with that one question: why had he abandoned me after I'd told him my husband was a criminal?

Thibault did his best to distract me, but after a text came back saying Léon would visit the next day at half past ten if that was convenient, I wanted to throw the phone against the wall. No, it was not convenient! I never wanted to see that man again!

So when the clock struck eleven the next day, and he still wasn't there, I almost whooped. It was eleven. He wasn't here. Too late! Case closed. And then he knocked. Of course he did. It was still eleven. I had hardly slept and I was miserable, but I had to answer the door. Dragging my feet, I moved through the hallway. Eyes closed. Deep breath. Reach for the handle.

2
Won't you come in?

I opened the door, and my cheeks warmed. It was him. The same him. Those eyes. That smile. I smiled back. How could I not? He was my friend.

'Where have you been?' My smile was still in place, but my eyes overflowed.

His smile cracked under the weight of the sadness in his brown eyes. He reached for me, and I let him envelop me, every mixed emotion I'd had throughout the night coming out in one big sob. I didn't know if seeing him made me so happy because it was him, or because of the realisation that seeing him meant that all the fear and anxiety I'd relived throughout the night were in the past. He was not a cactus. I could get close if I wanted to.

But did he want to? Was that why he was here, even after he'd abandoned me before?

For some reason, my mother's voice sounded in the back of my head, telling me to be a better hostess, but I shushed it. I needed this moment in Léon's arms before I could question him on his betrayal.

I breathed in his slightly dusty scent as I leaned my head against his shoulder. When I realised I'd never hugged him before, I pushed him away, embarrassed that I'd exposed all my feelings before he'd said one word.

'Won't you come in?' I tried to recover some of my dignity by making my words sound as formal as I could manage.

He didn't move. I didn't dare look him in the eye, but I heard him take in a breath as if he were going to speak. After a long pause he finally said, 'I was there. At the trial. I know you told me not to come, but I couldn't *not* be there.'

I stared at the top button of his beige shirt. How did he know about the trial? That was long after he'd left.

'I told you...?'

He nodded, ducking down to catch my gaze. 'You said you didn't want me involved. *Eh ben...* you'd said that about a million times before you ghosted me, but I had to be there. I'm sorry I didn't honour your wishes. But you never answered any of my calls. I had to know you'd be all right.'

I was looking at him, but I didn't see him. I saw Franck on trial. I saw him uttering his death threat. Had that made me 'all right'?

Also, *I* ghosted *him*? Slowly, Léon came back into focus only to fade again. He caught me when my knees buckled.

'Let's go inside.' One arm around my waist to support me, he guided me through my door and into my kitchen, where he settled me on a chair. Then he crouched down in front of me. 'I'm sorry, Julie. If I'd known my presence would upset you this much, I wouldn't have contacted you.'

'What do you mean, I ghosted you?' How could he say that? *He* was the one who never answered my messages. My foggy brain wouldn't let me think of anything else until this had been cleared up. Had he tried to contact me after all? Had Franck found out about him and blocked my phone? I knew he'd regularly checked my phone, so I'd been careful to delete any record of messages and calls, apart from Léon's number under the entry Cactus. I figured if there were no evidence of contact, the strange name wouldn't stand out. But maybe Franck had found a way after all.

'You stopped answering my messages and never picked up when I called you. I think that is what's called ghosting, nowadays.'

If I hadn't been so befuddled, I'd have smiled at my old-fashioned friend. His students kept him up to date, but he was never very confident using terms that didn't appear in a dictionary from 1950. However, as it was, his being obtuse annoyed me. 'I know that. But how did you know about the trial? You stopped answering *my* messages long before that.'

His turn to look confused. 'No, I didn't. I must confess, I was quite shaken up when you told me about your husband's practices, but it was you whose messages became more and more erratic. You said I shouldn't get involved, and that it would be better for me to stay away.'

'But the trial wasn't until a year later.'

'Of course.'

'So?'

'Don't you remember? Look, I'll show you.' He took out his phone and opened his messages, scrolling up when he'd reached my name. Then he handed the phone to me.

The date showed November, five years earlier. My confiding message about how I found out Franck was a criminal. But instead of the hollow message I'd told Beau about, there was a conversation, with Léon's initial messages conveying shock and later his advice and support. But he was right. My responses were short and muddled, sometimes overly emotional and grateful, at other moments distant and vague. There was one message with a bunch of emojis exclaiming my happiness at the finalisation of my divorce, followed by months of messages only from Léon. One more text from me explained how Franck had turned his fraud on my beauty blog, my sole means of income.

That had been his downfall because I went to the police. His threats had been wasted on me because he'd left me at rock bottom. I had nowhere left to go but up. Though I felt I'd moved sideways on that bedrock for quite some time.

My text also told Léon not to come to the trial, for his own protection. All the other messages were from Léon, until about a month after the trial. His last one read 'This sucks.' I stared at that one. The familiar one. The one I'd remembered. But if I'd received that one, it couldn't have been Franck intercepting my messages.

Why?

This was only a few years ago. How had I been able to forget all this and turn the blame on Léon? But I had. Faced with the evidence, I allowed faint memories to resurface that I'd pushed away for years. The fear, the stress, the worry for the one person who was still there for me. Shaking, I repressed those feelings again. Emptiness was better for now. I couldn't deal with them. Not yet. But I knew they were there. And now I could add guilt to them.

'I'm sorry,' I whispered.

He took my hands in his, the phone falling to the floor. 'Are you all right?'

I shrugged. Who knew? 'If you are, I will be.'

Léon gently squeezed my fingers. 'I only wish I could have been there for you. But you were determined to keep me out of your life. To be honest, I never expected to hear back after the text I sent yesterday. I was ecstatic to get your answer. Still am, despite... this. Can I... do something? Get you a tissue?'

I reached up to find my cheeks were wet; even the top of my dress was soaked. My mascara! I must look a mess! And with the most wonderful man in the world beside me. I jumped up to grab a tissue from the dresser around the corner in the living room. Léon wisely left me to blow my nose and fix my face, though all I had for a mirror was the shiny antique copper coffee pot.

Taking a deep, shaky breath, I returned to the kitchen. Léon had claimed my chair after retrieving his phone from the floor, but he got up when I entered the room. I attempted a smile to alleviate the concern on his face, but failed miserably.

'Coffee?' I tried instead.

'Thank you. Can I help?'

I waved him back into his chair. Making coffee would give me an excuse to keep my face away from him until it was less puffy. I must already be the charity case among his acquaintances, so I'd better try and keep up the few appearances I still had. 'So how did you know I was in Saint-Maurice?'

He huffed out an embarrassed laugh. 'I created a fake account on your online store, hoping you'd let your customers know what your plans for the future were. It was the only way I could think of to keep in touch without bothering you.'

I swallowed, leaning on the counter for support. 'You didn't bother me.' Even now I knew the truth about him, I couldn't remember why I shut him out. But I knew he would never have bothered me.

'I'm sorry,' I said again.

He didn't answer but came to stand beside me. When I turned my bowed head slightly, I could see he was looking out the window, his face relaxed.

'Do you think we could start over?'

His eyes still on the outside world, he smiled. 'No. I don't want to pretend nothing has happened.' He turned towards me and lifted my chin. 'But I'd like to get back to us being friends, like before.'

Through the tears that were already welling up again, I looked at him. A smile was still too much to ask, but I nodded. Then I quickly got back to making coffee and hiding my face.

He reached for me, hesitated, and rubbed my arm instead, whatever his intent had been. Maybe I was still a cactus. Or maybe the situation was just weird. I should stop thinking in terms of cactuses. With Franck out of the way, there was no reason for me not to get close to Léon. If he felt the same. He said he wanted to get back to the way things were. But he'd said friends because that's what we were. We'd never been anything more. But who says we couldn't be?

I took a deep breath for courage and turned around, the coffee mugs gripped tightly. If he was going to be my friend, he should learn to deal with my blotchy face. Yes, I know it was *me* who would have to learn to show him my blotchy face, but I was feeling rough, so I granted myself a little self-deception.

'So why are you in Saint-Maurice? And don't say to visit me because you said yourself that you didn't expect a reply.'

'My girlfriend's father lives here, so we're visi...'

He kept talking, but I didn't hear. I stared at him. Did he not hear the whole building crumbling to the ground around us? Mentally, I kicked myself. I had never considered a romantic involvement after Franck, except maybe just this moment, so why would Léon have spent years pining for me with no encouragement? Friends, remember? But my heart still hurt.

'She really wants to meet you.'

Who? Oh, the girlfriend, of course.

'So I thought I'd better find out if you wanted to see me at all.'

'Don't be silly. Of course I do.' Well, I did now. Not so sure about her, though.

'Excellent. Will you come and have lunch with us? I heard the food in your café is *magnifique*.'

'Us? Who's us?' Thibault strolled into the kitchen as if he owned it.

Léon did a double take, looked at me, then back at Beau, but said nothing other than, 'Good morning.'

I thought it prudent to make some introductions. 'Léon, this is my assistant, Thibault Fouquet. Beau, Léon Levotre.'

Léon frowned at the mention of Beau's last name, so I hastened to add, 'Franck's nephew, but he hates Franck almost as much as I do.'

Léon stood to shake Beau's hand, while Beau did not disguise his suspicion of the newcomer. In fact, when he saw my face, he puffed up like a blond cockerel. 'What do you want?'

'Beau...' I started, but Léon smiled.

'I'm a friend, I assure you. As are you, undoubtedly. In which case, the invitation to lunch extends to you too. Will you join me and my girlfriend at your local bistro?'

Beau never let an opportunity like that pass, so the fact that he hesitated spoke volumes.

'We'd be delighted,' I lied. I had no desire to meet this girlfriend, but I wanted the two most important men in my life to get along.

'Excellent,' Léon repeated. 'I'll call Véronique to meet us there.'

He went into the hallway to make the call, and Beau pounced on the opportunity. 'Are you okay?'

At his worried frown, I produced a watery smile. 'What I remembered about him was wrong. He did help. It's just... memories. You know?'

He crouched down in front of my chair like Léon had done before, but he'd been around long enough to know to hug me.

Léon returned to the kitchen, and Beau let go, but his raised eyebrows asked me, 'Are you sure?'

Squeezing his arm, I got up. 'I'll go freshen up.'

Whatever happened between the two of them in the fifteen minutes I needed to make myself presentable – he might have a girlfriend, but that didn't mean I shouldn't make an effort for my old friend – by the time I entered the kitchen once more, they were laughing at some joke or other. Seeing the two men together like that did more for my mood than anything either of them could have said.

'You ready?' I asked.

They looked at each other and laughed, but even that couldn't annoy me.

3

The Woman in the Wine

The short walk to the village centre left me exhausted. This morning's emotional rediscovery had drained me. Véronique turned out to be everything I was not: tall, slim, a blonde that might even be natural, and – on the surface at least – emotionally stable. If Léon had a type, I was not it. But since he already had her, I needn't concern myself with t hat.

As soon as she saw us, the girlfriend zoomed towards me with an outstretched hand. 'Julie. I've heard so much about you.' The perfect blend of politeness and warmth in her voice, she was one of the most likeable people I'd ever met. I instantly disliked her.

While we waited for our orders, I sat through the necessary small talk, my head pounding throughout. I hadn't realised Véronique was the daughter of Gilles de Vigan, the owner of the local wine bar, but now I was glad Thibault was there to nod along and smile, so I could rudely ponder her age – I knew Léon was a few years older than me, but she must be pushing forty – and what it was she'd heard about me. I didn't have to wait long.

'And one of the first things my father told me when I came back was that they'd had another murder in the village, and that you'd caught the killer.'

'What do you mean, another?' Beau asked. 'The one here in the village came first, *then* the one in the château.'

Véronique shook her head. 'No, I meant the unsolved one. The Woman in the Wine? That was my mother.'

She paused, playing with the stem of her wine glass, while I studied her. I'd heard about this case from my own mother. That murder had happened before my parents were even married, so more than thirty-three years ago. Véronique must have been very young at the time. Though it had been a lifetime ago, I still felt for her. It also embarrassed me that I'd secretly been trying to find negative things about her.

'That's... kind of why I wanted to meet you.' She kept her gaze on the wine glass. 'Since you're apparently good at solving these kinds of mysteries, I thought, maybe...' When she looked up, her eyes pleaded with me. 'Maybe you could look into my mother's case?'

I recoiled, and she reached over the table for my hand, which I withdrew reflexively.

'I could pay you! There's nothing—'

'What makes you think I can do what a whole team of police people couldn't when everything was still fresh in people's memories?' If it hadn't been for Léon, I would have stood up and walked away. Every instinct screamed at me to stay away from this murder. My mother had told me how it had upset the whole village for months while the investigation was ongoing, but that it had been even worse when no murderer could be identified. Why would I want to poke around in dusty files that wouldn't reveal anything new? On top of that, Véronique was obviously still very emotional about the matter. She'd be scrutinising my every move and would probably be gutted when she'd have to give up on finding justice for her mother's killer all over again.

'Won't you try?'

I shook my head.

'Please?'

That's when I caught sight of Léon. He hadn't said a thing since Véronique mentioned her mother. His expression was oddly blank, which I took to mean that he didn't want to influence my decision. Grateful as I was for that, my guilt immediately took over. I'd shut him out and falsely blamed him for years. Now that we'd reconnected, I couldn't very well deny him my help the moment he asked for it, could I? Okay, so it was his girlfriend doing the asking. But what kind of friend would I be if I didn't at least appear to be willing to help?

I closed my eyes and rubbed my temples. 'Do you have any reason other than pure hope to believe I could make a difference? It's been over thirty years. Has something changed that makes you think I could find new evidence?'

Her shoulders sagged. 'Well... no. Maybe. I'm not sure. Not yet anyway.'

Ah, yes, that sounded promising. 'And if you do know something that wasn't considered at the time, why don't you look into it yourself?'

'I advised her not to.'

I raised my eyebrows at Léon.

'She's too close to this. The emotional impact of talking to people who wouldn't be able to give her any closure would be devastating.'

My gaze flitted between the two. Did that mean he'd only come to me for my reputation? That he hadn't really cared to renew our friendship after all?

'In fact, I advised her to find any other way to deal with the matter. I know several therapists who—'

'I don't need therapy!'

Hmm... Was she sure about that?

'I need to know who killed my mother. Someone got away with murder! How can you not care about that?'

Before the situation could get out of hand, I donned my blue helmet. 'I can't guarantee I'll find anything at all. Especially if you have no new leads to give me.' What was I doing?

Thibault's lips twitched. His eyes were already sparkling at the prospect of another investigation, but my heart sank.

Léon looked me in the eye. 'You don't have to do this, Julie.'

Good. If I didn't have to do it for him, I certainly didn't owe his girlfriend anything. I opened my mouth, but he wasn't finished.

'But if you're set on shining your light on whatever you can find out, I think we should promise not to push you if you hit a dead end.' He said this more to Véronique than to me, but I felt the words prod me into unwilling action.

She crossed her arms in front of her, but then seemed to let go of her defiance and nodded.

Our food arrived, and for several minutes the others all ate in silence. I stabbed at the sea bream on my plate, but my throat felt thick and scratchy, and though I'd tried to pick something soft, I still didn't want to swallow any more than I had to. Of course, the fish looked and smelled delicious, making my mouth water, so I had to swallow anyway. Might as well make some food go down with it.

Léon remarked on the quality of the food, which set off another bout of polite small talk. Having finished the fish with difficulty, I declined dessert, earning me some serious side-eye from Beau. But without food to concentrate on, the meal seemed to last even longer. Eventually, though, the torture was over and we said our goodbyes, having thanked Léon for lunch.

We had only made it to the door, when a voice stopped me.

'Juju!' Jeanette, the owner of the café, hurried between the tables to catch us. 'Could you... Oh. You don't look too good. I was going to ask you for a favour, but I think you should go to bed instead.'

Yay for friends who tell you the truth to your face.

I waved her concerns away. 'It's all right. If I can help, I'd love to. What do you need?'

She hesitated but was obviously also itching to ask. 'If you're sure... I found an old picture in amongst some papers that were left at the hotel. Do you have time to come look at it?' She pointed over my shoulder across the square.

Even with its prime location within the village, the hotel had been empty for decades. I wondered what she could have found. 'Just for the picture?'

She nodded, and I glanced at Beau, who shrugged.

'Après toi.'

Jeanette hurried to the hotel's side entrance, ushering us inside before quickly closing the door again. She rubbed her arms since she hadn't bothered to put on a coat, but the hotel lobby was no warmer than outside.

From the moment we'd bought the place, Jeanette had spent every bit of spare time in here, clearing out and making plans. Her ideas were amazing but costly, and even with my investment, she'd still had to apply for loans and grants. Most of them had now been either approved or declined, so it wouldn't be long until the renovations could start. In fact, we were scheduled to have a meeting with the contractor the next day at eleven.

While Jeanette ducked behind the 1970s-style reception desk, which was clad in wooden slats, I made my usual round of the lobby, brushing against the brown pleather tub chairs, imagining all the changes Jeanette had in mind. Straightening a large oil painting of a vase of flowers, I took in the modernist mural beside it. Fortunately, that monstrosity would be one of the first things to go. I'm sure some people like that kind of abstract stuff, but let's just say it was not to my taste. And since it also didn't go with Jeanette's plans, it was out.

'Aha!' Jeanette rose from behind the reception desk. She held up an envelope and produced a faded and stained photograph of the hotel's lobby. 'I know it's in a state, but since you do photos, I thought maybe you could have a look at it and see if you could, you know, make it better somehow?'

I took the picture with a frown. 'This kind of thing needs a specialist.'

She pouted. 'Yes, I was afraid of that. But I didn't want to spend your money on that right now. I guess it'll have to wait.' She sighed.

'I could... scan it and see what I can do digitally?' I offered. Very, very reluctantly.

But her face lighting up was what I did it for.

'You're such a push-over,' Beau declared as we were walking home.

'I like to see people happy,' I corrected him.

'You know how you told me I could stay for the night three months ago?'

'Good of you to remind me. When are you leaving?'

He only grinned widely.

As we strolled past what I still thought of as the Durands' house, a young woman with pink hair in her early twenties waved cheerfully at me from inside. I waved back, pasting on my best fake smile. My head was still filled with moody reminiscences and regret over having accepted two projects that would give me no pleasure to fulfil, especially with the way my head was pounding. I was not in the mood to give an exuberant welcome. But since this pink-haired young woman was probably my new neighbour, I didn't want to leave her with the impression that I was the village curmudgeon. Especially with Beau beside me, giving his happy-puppy wave. If he'd had a tail, he'd have been wagging it off.

We'd already passed the new neighbour's house when she came out, carrying a heavy cardboard box. Thibault rushed to take it from her.

'Oh! Thank you. I was just taking it to the carport.'

'Carrying heavy things is usually easier in more practical shoes, you know.' He said it with a wink and his trademark swoon-worthy smile, which prevented anyone from ever getting angry with him. Except maybe his mum.

The woman, however, was not his mum, so she flicked her pink locks and giggled. 'These are actually the most practical I own.' The platform wedge trainers were edgy, but decidedly not up to the job. 'I get all my clothes from brands I represent. Are you from around here?'

'We live on the other side of the pasture.' Beau waved in the direction of my house.

The woman's face lit up. 'That's great! I throw a lot of parties, so consider yourself invited. You too, of course,' she added to me as an afterthought.

Beau seemed to be happy with it, but I wondered if she'd be the loud music type. My clients were always going on about the peaceful location. Though it wasn't what I advertised or what they came for, it would be a shame to lose it.

The woman had climbed onto a stack of unpacked boxes and was trying to flatten them. 'Whenever I move, there's always that moment I hope my new neighbours catch, where

I'm doing something amazing, and they might think, "Ooh, she's quite strong". What they actually see is moments like these – The Amazing Human *Presse-Papier* – and the only thing they can think is, "Ooh, she's quite heavy"...'

Laughing, Thibault introduced us and we shook hands in an awkward vertical fashion.

'I'm Anne-Bonny. Like the pirate?'

I shrugged while Beau helped her climb down from the cardboard mound. 'I don't know much about pirates.'

'So the other day I saw this documentary on pirates, right. It was so old, like from the 1920s, so, you know, the actual days of the pirates. I never knew people used to walk so funny! Kind of made me rethink how cool my name was, but I can't change it now. Unless I do, like, a full Prince.'

We both laughed with her, but to be honest, my laugh was more in astonishment than actual mirth. After we'd said goodbye and good luck with the unpacking, Thibault grinned at m e.

'She's not going to be your customer, right?' He was referring to my rule of not sleeping with anyone who was, is, or ever will be my client.

'Beau, no! Down boy. She's my neighbour. She does not need you.' Referring to his 'rule' of needing him to get him. Whatever that meant.

'I think you're right, she needs a professional.'

Shaking my head, I gave him a scolding look. 'She may not get her history right, but that's no reason to write her off. I thought she was funny. And she may bring more people your age to the area. Although I too, of course, was invited to her parties.'

'Don't get your petticoats in a twist, *ma tigre*. You're only nine years older. I'm sure she didn't mean anything by that. It's just me.' He spread his arms wide. 'I'm blinding. I'm so dazzling that I take up people's complete attention. You've no idea how much effort it takes me to not be overwhelming when you're with your clients.'

'Hm, yes, I should pay you damages, really.'

He closed his eyes and beat his heart with his fist. 'Your acknowledgement of my pain soothes my cramped ego.'

Grinning at him sideways, I toyed with several remarks about the size of his ego and how easily it would be cramped, but in the end it was, 'Too easy.'

'Me? How dare you. Even I have standards, you know.'

'We'll have to look for them one day.'

Surprisingly, meeting Anne-Bonny and the subsequent exchange with Beau had boosted my mood. Since he was always so eager to play detective, perhaps it was time to give him a bigger role in the upcoming investigation. That thought alone made me hate it a little bit less.

As soon as we got home and I had my hands wrapped around a cup of tea with plenty of honey, I called my mother. As the mayor of Saint-Maurice, Flora Belmain would have the best access to any files relating to the ancient murder case. Was I really a pushover? Either that, or people liked to play off my curiosity, and I knew I wasn't the curious kind. Boy, I hated when Beau might be right. I decided then and there to grow a backbone and say 'no' more often.

'*Salut, ma belle,*' my mum sang into the phone. Wednesdays were her days off, so she was probably crocheting something intricate and delicate.

'Hi, Mum,' I rasped, clearing my painful throat. 'Quick question – can I access the files on the Woman in the Wine?'

My mother remained silent for a beat. 'Not through me. They're police files. Why are you interested in them? Haven't you had enough of murder already?'

I couldn't blame her for questioning my sanity. 'Véronique de Vigan. She asked me to "look into it".' I was sure my mother could hear my quotation marks.

'And you didn't think to say no?'

Not at the time, I grumbled to myself.

Maman sighed. 'Of course you didn't. This isn't going to lead anywhere, *chérie*. But if you need my help, I'm here.'

4
Maybe it's still too soon

Three decades earlier

The stone hovered in front of Flora's eyes. It was connected to a ring, in a box, held open by a kneeling young man. The man she loved. Flora stared at the man, who now waited for her answer with eyes so full of a trusting love that left her almost no room to say no. And yet...

The man seemed to realise no answer was coming. 'I know you think I'm impulsive, even though it's been two years. Maybe it's still too soon. You don't have to give me your answer now, but... I love you. This is what I want. You, as my wife.'

Flora could only stare some more. That, and swallow and blink. But no coherent thoughts formed in her head, and therefore, no coherent words came out of her mouth.

Nicolas Belmain got up, chuckled, and pecked her on the cheek. 'I'm sorry, *chérie*. I thought you might be ready to make the decision, but I've only added to the stress.' He pulled her in for a cuddle that felt so right, but also very strange after what had just happened.

She slowly became aware of her surroundings again. The modest flat had surprised her when they first got together. She'd known him, of course. They came from the same village of under 1,200 people, and he was the son of the mayor. The Belmains were old money, so she'd expected him to live somewhere more grand, more up to the standards he must be used to. But, as he'd told her, he didn't need more than this. She'd fallen a little bit more in love with him then and there. Now, two years later, he'd been looking at the kind of house she'd expected in the first place, joking that they'd raise their kids in splendour. At least, she thought he'd been joking.

'Unless your answer is yes or no right now, I don't mind waiting,' he said into her hair.

'It's not no…' she said at last, which earned her a soft squeeze.

'I knew it wouldn't be.'

But would it never be no? Him, she'd marry in a heartbeat. He must know that. But he'd made it clear that he took his obligations to the village seriously. What he meant was that in Saint-Maurice, his family had been in charge for centuries, and nobody had ever questioned that. Through revolutions and wars, the titles and rules of possession had changed, but when it came to leadership, the entire village still looked to the Belmains. The two were inextricably linked. Marrying Nicolas would be like marrying the village. And Flora wasn't at all sure she could handle that.

Nicolas seemed unperturbed, chatting happily as he let her go and went into the tiny kitchen. 'When you do say yes, we wouldn't have to get married right away, of course. We could travel. See the world first, before duty would keep us here.'

He went on to name all the places he wanted to visit, but Flora squeezed her eyes shut. She didn't need to see the world. She had everything she wanted right here in Saint-Maurice. But that's because she chose to be here. What he proposed meant being stuck here. Even if she'd never have left of her own accord, not having the option would be stifling.

Then again, if she said no, she'd effectively ban herself from Saint-Maurice. She couldn't live in a village where everyone knew she'd turned down their leader. Without meaning to, Nicolas had given her a choice. Stay or leave, but either choice would be permanent.

Suddenly needing fresh air, Flora dashed from the flat without saying goodbye. She felt bad leaving Nicolas like that, but he'd started it. Once outside, she took a deep breath and shivered despite the late summer sun. She didn't get long to recover, though.

'Ah, Flo! I was looking for you. What do you think, the green or the yellow?' Lily Ta hurried towards her with a catalogue in her hands. This was a regular occurrence, so Flora knew it wouldn't take long. Lily was terrible at making decisions, especially when it came to life events like her wedding and now preparing for her first baby. While Flora had tried to get her to make her own choices by making lists of pros and cons, she'd learned that in the end, it was easier to let Lily narrow things down to two choices, and then to simply choose herself. If Lily found that she liked the other option better, she would go for that one after all. Today's options were between a vanilla-yellow or mint-green baby cot.

'Yellow,' was all she managed, but it was enough.

Lily beamed at her. 'I knew it! You're a treasure. *Merci!*'

Flora smiled as Lily hurried back home. She couldn't possibly leave this village. Whatever would Lily do for choices? Her new husband, much as he adored her, only ever shrugged and said that she should do whatever made her happy. But maybe Flora could simply instruct him a little before she left?

Trudging along the street on a busy Saturday morning, she ended up at the Place de l'Église, the village square. Around the hotel, people were setting up for the *concours culinaire* that was to take place the next day. Every year, Saint-Maurice hosted a cooking contest to see who could make the best *saucisson au gène*, a traditional Beaujolais delicacy. Flora didn't like the contest much. It was one of the biggest things happening in the village and attracted lots of people to the local businesses. In terms of advertisement for the Saint-Maurice wineries, you couldn't get much better than this, with both wine and food connoisseurs coming in from far and wide to taste the regional goodness.

But the whole thing turned the villagers mad. Where ordinarily you could ask anyone for anything, and they'd be honoured to help you out, around contest time, it was every man and woman for themselves.

'Can you give me a hand, Flora?'

Ugh, the worst offender in the category Looking Out for Number One, Louanne de Vigan. Then again, she was like that all the time. Her self-importance only increased during the competition, albeit about a thousand times. Part of it might be justified, as she'd won for years in a row, but the way she bossed people around was intolerable.

'Absolutely, what do you need?'

'I've recruited some of the teenage girls to hand out flyers in Villefranche. They're inside. Can you show them where they can find the boxes?'

'Sure—'

'And then drive them to Villefranche? Thanks!'

Before Flora could answer, Louanne carried her shoulder pads up a ladder to reattach a giant banner to the front of the hotel. Flora shut her mouth with a snap. She wanted to be distracted? Well, she got what she asked for. And with Nicolas proposing and her now not wanting to see him, most of her plans went out the window, so in fact, she did have time to chauffeur the girls around. Grinding her teeth, she entered the hotel lobby through the revolving doors.

Built in the 1930s, the hotel retained some or its original art deco features, but it had been extensively redecorated about fifteen years before. The shiny marble floor was now covered with a burnt-orange carpet, and the painted tiles Flora remembered from her childhood had been covered with plasterboard to give the lobby a sleek, modern look. Unfortunately, with design harking back to art deco the last few years, what had been stylish only a decade ago now already looked dated.

The girls Flora was to drive weren't hard to find. They were at one end of the reception desk that stretched along the left wall, talking to a man who had his back to Flora. One of the girls was behind him, showing only her permed, teased, and hairsprayed fringe, extending high above the man's shoulder. The other girl Flora knew only as Apolline.

'Hi, Cédric,' Flora greeted the receptionist. 'Mind if I squeeze by to get the boxes of flyers?'

'Oh, you've been roped into doing it, then? Figures.' The gangly student rolled his eyes behind his giant glasses.

Flora shrugged as she knelt behind the reception desk.

'Can't stand the woman.' The mumbled words were so familiar, Flora didn't pay much attention. Where she sat, Apolline's voice drowned out Cédric's anyway.

'I have a friend in Villefranche who's into that sort of thing, so I know all about it. She's friends with Luc Leduc, you know,' Apolline said.

The man with her answered in an appreciative voice. 'He's certainly one to keep an eye on. Very avant-garde. Though I myself prefer the organic lines of Esmeralda Quimper. Her sculptures are very good too.'

Flora had found the boxes and dragged them forward.

Cédric took them from her and slid them towards the girls. '*Tenez, les filles.* Time to get to work.'

Rounding the reception desk, Flora rattled her car keys. 'I'll drop you off near the *marché couvert*. That's the busiest place on market day.'

Both girls said goodbye to the man, who nodded a greeting to Flora. She smiled back and waved at Cédric before joining the girls outside.

'I'm surprised he even knows Luc Leduc,' Apolline was telling her hairsprayed friend. 'Maybe he's not as bad as I thought.'

'Good luck!' came a voice from above. Perched on the top rung of the ladder, Louanne wielded a hammer with such a loose grip that Flora herded the girls out of the danger zone.

'Did you know she's having an affair with Monsieur Prunille?' the hairsprayed friend asked Apolline when they were out of earshot.

'No!'

'Yes!'

High-pitched giggling ensued, making Flora's skin crawl. 'Spreading unsubstantiated rumours is not a wise thing to do.' She sounded like her mother. Maybe her mother had been right.

The girls rolled their eyes and continued giggling, only at a slightly less jarring frequency. This was going to be a long trip.

5

Gilles thinks it's unhealthy

I coughed to get rid of the tickle in my throat, but now my lungs hurt. Gilles de Vigan was an old man. I shouldn't be talking to him with my brewing cold. That was my excuse, at least, for not acting on my apparent promise to investigate Véronique's mother's death. Honestly, what did she expect? That I'd pull a killer out of the hat like some demented Fabien le Fabuleux? Because other than with magic, there was no way I was going to suddenly solve a thirty-year-old murder case. Even the recent ones had been largely down to luck, but this case had been examined by many people more capable than me, and none of them had come up with a solution.

I pulled the sleeves of my chunky-knit jumper over my hands and enveloped my hot tisane. Sage, thyme, and rose-hip with a dollop of honey would hopefully boost my immune system enough. If not, I'd have to go for the bigger guns, but ginger and turmeric were not my go-to flavours. For now, I snuggled down on the fluffy throw that covered the scratch marks on my sofa. The miscreant responsible for those marks had come in from the cold and lay curled up at my feet, purring away.

With a sigh, I scratched Henri behind his ear and pulled my laptop towards me. I'd already done an online search for the murder, but there wasn't much more than what I already knew. I opened a document and wrote down some bullet points.

1. The victim: Louanne de Vigan. Married to Gilles de Vigan. One daughter, Véronique, who was six years old at the time. Cooking champion. Not very well liked.

2. Scene of the crime: one of Auguste's wine vats.

My fingers hovered over the keyboard. Technically, Auguste was my neighbour on both sides. His house and winery were on the downhill side, but he also owned the field surrounding the house of my new pink-haired neighbour. And then, of course, the vineyards on the other side of our little valley, facing south, were mostly his too. There were plenty of jokes going round the village about Auguste's wine being so good because literal blood, sweat, and tears went into it. Or that one where they'd asked him if he'd ever make bad wine and he'd said 'over my dead body', but nobody realised he'd meant he had someone else's dead body there.

You'd think a dead body in your wine vat would ruin your business, wouldn't you? But strangely, Auguste had fared well by it. He'd had a rock-solid alibi for the night it happened, so instead of blame, he got sympathy, and everyone chipped in to save him from ruin. I smiled. Auguste was a complete and utter dear and he deserved nothing less. But the question remained – how and why did a dead body end up in one of his wine vats?

3. Suspects: ...

I hammered out the dots with abandon. Other than those dots, I had no suspects. The story of the Woman in the Wine was more of an anecdote than a detailed news story, so while everyone knew the basics, nobody ever talked about what exactly had happened.

'Find out who did it yet?' My partner in crime solving breezed in, munching on a pear.

'You're dripping on my parquet! Get a plate or a bowl or something.'

He shrugged, licked his wrist, and perched on the armrest beside me, peering at my screen. 'That's not a lot.'

'Thank you for your observation. *Quelle nouille,*' I muttered.

'So what did happen?'

I grunted, wincing at the subsequent pain in my throat. 'That's what I'm trying to remember, obviously. But since this all happened before I was born, I only have a vague grasp of the facts. All I know is that a woman was found face down in one of the presses. You know, one of those old-fashioned ones they used for treading the grapes? They searched for weeks, but they never found the killer.'

'So...' Thibault frowned at my computer screen. 'This was what, thirty odd years ago? Did they still press the grapes manually then? Or whatever it's called when you do it with your feet?'

'Actually, Auguste lets his grapes ferment whole. You get fewer tannins that way, so a very light wine. But they used that press after the *vendanges*. Everyone who'd helped pick the grapes was invited to a big celebration, where they pressed some grapes in there as a kind of party game. Auguste got rid of his after the whole murder business, but I know some other people around here still use old presses for that purpose. It's just for fun.'

Beau busted out some dance moves. 'Par-tay! You people sure know how to entertain.'

Apparently, our traditions were wasted on the city boy. I threw him a withering look as he continued dripping, albeit on his own jeans this time.

'I should probably talk to Véronique's father. He'll know all there is to know, but I don't want to give him my cold.' And by the time I got better, Léon might have convinced Véronique that it'd be better if she let it rest.

'I can go, if you want? I'll call you, and you can hear every-thing he has to say and ask your own questions, but it won't be as impersonal as if you'd simply called him.'

I hated when Beau did that. Just when I'd reasoned myself into not having to do something, he took the wind out of my sails with his blasted kindness and logic. I sipped my tisane to postpone my answer another few seconds.

'I don't want to bother you with it.' But I knew what was coming.

He jumped up, the remains of the pear squished in his fist. 'No bother at all. When was your next client, again?'

'End of next week. It's January, slow season for photog-raphers. I've only got a few Christmas presents booked in. Hopefully I'll feel better by then.' I coughed to show him the sorry state I was in, but regretted it immediately. Sorry indeed.

The perky assistant hadn't even noticed. Or if he had, he'd decided not to give my self-pity any attention. 'Where does he live, Monsieur de Vigan?'

I explained, and he left. I pouted at Henri, but he had his face turned the other way and took no notice. Men!

'Gilles thinks it's unhealthy.'

My brain needed a few seconds to process that, since as soon as Beau had left, I'd fallen asleep. He must have been talking to Véronique's father on his own before calling me, since this didn't feel like waking up from a cat nap. 'Why?'

'*Alors*, little bit of background that he's given, that Véronique failed to mention. She's been living abroad for the past twenty years or so. Never mentions her mother, never seemed to care much. She was sad, of course, after her mum died, but Gilles says they made it work together, and she's never expressed any sort of wish to know what happened. He thinks she should let it rest, and that it's not going to bring her anything good.'

So far, so good for my wish to stay out of the whole mess. 'Doesn't he want to know what happened?'

'He says he did at the time, but he's made peace with not knowing. So I'll give you to him now.'

I quickly checked my own video image to see if my nap hadn't destroyed my hairstyle or left a mark on my face, but I was still presentable.

The wavy white hair of Gilles de Vigan appeared on the screen, followed by wrinkled eyes and finally the smile that had created all those wrinkles. 'This is the first time I've called anyone but Véronique this way. *Salut*, Julie, good to see you. I hear you're a bit under the weather.'

I smiled apologetically. I only knew the old man as the owner of the village *caveau*, and I'd seen him behind the counter at the wine bar, but as he was far past retirement age, he wasn't there very often.

'Very good of you to think of my health. I appreciate that. Your friend here explained that Roni has asked you about her mother.'

I nodded. 'But I don't know anything about what happened that night, so I thought I'd talk to you first. I'm sorry if all this brings back bad memories.'

Gilles shrugged one shoulder. 'It's not your fault. But I think it will be a fairly short adventure. For all I know, she was just at the wrong place at the wrong time, and someone completely unrelated to the village or its goings-on killed her by accident.'

'By drowning her in a wine press?'

'They never could discover signs of force. She'd had a lot to drink. There was an open press with fermenting grapes. Carbon dioxide, you know? Maybe she fell.' He sighed, looking away from the camera. 'She was quite a difficult woman, as I'm sure you've heard. But let me start at the beginning. You know about the *concours culinaire* they used to have?'

I nodded, but I heard Beau say no, so I explained, 'Saint-Maurice used to host an immensely popular cooking contest that amateurs could join. They all made the same local dish, *saucisson au gène*, but what they put in the sausage, how they prepared the grape-skin sauce, what accompaniment they added – those were the choices that could make or break them.'

'Louanne was obsessed with it.' Gilles took over. 'This all happened in the run-up to the contest, so she'd been organising the event and cooking the saucisson this way and that to perfect her recipe. It was a really stressful time for her. And for us, to be honest. Véronique was only six at the time, but around contest time, Louanne sent her to her grandmother – my mother-in-law – for a few weeks, so she could concentrate on the competition. I didn't agree with that decision, but Louanne was... a very headstrong woman. I'm ashamed to say I was no match for her. If she wanted something, she got it. I loved that about her,' he added with a rueful smile.

'I can't really tell you much about what happened. Because of the pressure surrounding the competition, Louanne had drunk more wine than usual that night, and she went out to "clear her head", in her words. But she never came home. I think it was around ten o'clock I got a little worried, but more about her having stumbled and fallen somewhere. I went outside to try and find her, but they found me instead. The police. Then I got really worried, but it was already too late. They'd found her hanging over the edge of Auguste's stomping vat.'

'The police found her?' Beau asked off-screen.

'No, his wife. Auguste's wife. Claudine. Apparently, she'd screamed so loud, they could hear her in the village.'

'So… they never found out what happened?' Though I knew the answer, I could hardly believe it. In a village as small as Saint-Maurice, someone should have seen something.

He shrugged and shook his head half-heartedly.

'Why did she go to Claudine? Were they friends?'

'No!' It came out on a snort. 'Rivals. Almost enemies. Claudine was also set on winning the contest. She accused Louanne of cheating but could never prove it. I mean, how do you cheat in a cooking contest? Put drugs in your sausage?'

Beau chuckled.

I frowned. 'But if they didn't like each other, and Louanne was found in Claudine's press, wasn't Claudine a suspect?'

'*Bien sûr*. But any marks they found on Louanne's body were ambiguous, and even in an inebriated state, Louanne would have put up a fight. In the end, it was decided Claudine simply didn't have the strength to pull it off. Frankly, I never believed Claudine to be a murderer. Who would kill another person over a cooking contest?'

'So what do you think happened?' Beau asked.

Gilles shrugged again. 'Like I said, wrong place, wrong time. Perhaps she surprised a burglar. Or, for all I know, someone actually came for Claudine and lost their nerve after it turned out they'd killed the wrong person.'

'Why would anyone kill Claudine?'

'I don't know! Why would anyone kill my Louanne?' Gilles must have made a wide gesture after his outburst because the screen showed a blur of sleek furniture, walls with colourful things on them, and ceiling. When Gilles came back into view, he rubbed his face. '*Désolé.* I don't usually get upset about it any more. And I'm sorry Véronique brought it up after all these years. As I told Thibault, she went to the States to study and remained there. Now that she's found a job here, she's suddenly determined to find her mother's killer. I wish she would let it go. Apart from the fact that she lost her mother, and I the love of my life, we've had good lives as a family of two. As far as we know, nobody else was hurt, and the village has managed without Louanne.

'To be honest, Julie, I wish you hadn't promised to help. Roni is just wasting everyone's time. But she won't listen. Not to me, not to Léon... She's her mother's daughter all right.' He sighed and stared over the top of the phone.

'I'm sorry you feel that way, Gilles.' I didn't know the man very well, but I felt for him. Losing your wife was bad enough, especially if it involved violence, but to have the wound torn open after more than thirty years, and by your own child... I couldn't imagine what he was going through. 'I can't go back on my word, but I already told Véronique that I probably won't find anything. So hopefully it won't take too long before she has to accept that there's nothing anyone can do.'

He nodded, looking worn and older than he'd done at the beginning of our conversation.

'Is there anything you can give me to speed up my research? Friends, enemies...?'

He shook his head so lightly that it could have been the phone moving. 'People get intimidated by a strong character. She didn't have many friends. I wouldn't call any of the people she dealt with enemies, really, but she wasn't well liked. Other than Roni and me, I don't think anyone missed her.'

I thanked him and said goodbye, leaving Thibault to deal with cheering the old man up a bit before he left. Beau being Beau, I knew I could count on him to do just that. I sat staring at the empty spot on the fuzzy blanket where Henri had been before I fell asleep. My laptop was there, too, complete with empty list of suspects. Could I add anyone at all?

The only person Gilles had mentioned was Claudine, Auguste's wife. But she had passed away last year. I could, of course, ask Auguste, but after witnessing Gilles's distress, I didn't want another old man upset about the loss of his wife.

I picked up the phone and sent a text to Jacqueline, my friend with the Villefranche police force.

What do I have to do for you to show me 30-year-old police files about an unsolved murder?

I already dreaded her response. It could go either of two ways: a simple no, or a tirade about how could I possibly expect her to break the rules, and did I want her fired, blah, blah, blah.

In order not to sit and wait for Jacquie to answer, I called my mother.

'I don't have long, Juju. I have to leave for an... appointment in ten.'

Ignoring that intriguing, uncharacteristic vagueness for now, I rattled off my question. 'Apart from Claudine, do you know anyone else who could have been involved?'

She was silent for quite a long time. I was already checking my phone to see if I'd lost the connection, when she said, 'That is a very difficult question. You know I don't gossip.'

'And I don't listen to gossip. But I have to start somewhere.'

'Let me think about this and I'll come by after... my appointment.' She hung up, and I was left still staring at my phone and waiting for Jacquie to answer.

Léon had better appreciate my efforts. Not that I'd done all that much yet, but everything I had done, had been against my will. It would have been different if Léon had been in favour of me investigating this case. With him cheering me on, I'd have found the killer already. Well, as soon as Jacquie had provided me with the information I needed, of course. On cue, my phone pinged.

Unsolved cases are now public access. What do you need?

I stared at my phone. Could it be that easy? *Anything you have on the Woman in the Wine, please. Louanne de Vigan, found dead in Saint-Maurice in a wine press.*

She answered with a thumbs-up, and I smiled at my living room. This would be easy! I could do all my sleuthing from my nice, warm couch. For my cockiness, I was rewarded with a coughing fit that convinced me to break out the ginger and turmeric.

6

Let's move to Southern California

I had just finished scanning Jeanette's old photograph into my computer, when Thibault came back from his visit to Gilles.

'What a nice man.'

I smiled at Beau's unexpected contentment. 'Yeah? Did he stroke your ego? Or your little blond head?'

'Ha, ha. Seriously. He was hospitable and interested. Much more than just civil. Some people have their judgement ready as soon as they see my bike. Good or bad. But he waited to hear what I had to say without jumping to conclusions. In my experience, that's pretty rare.'

Little Beau had a new hero. I was happy for him, of course, but I also couldn't help feeling amused at seeing the stars in his eyes. 'Maybe running a wine bar all your life helps you reserve judgement. I've never really talked to him before, but it's good to know decent people still exist.'

Beau nodded in agreement, then pointed at my screen. 'Think you can do anything with that?'

I huffed. 'Hardly. It needs a good clean, but all my equipment is digital. I did do a course on film photography last year, though, and I've stayed in contact with the teacher. I'm going to send them this and see what they think.' I drained my cup of ginger and turmeric tea. 'But I don't expect to hear from them today. It's already getting dark.'

'It's only four.'

I checked the clock on the computer screen. 'I hate winter. Let's move to Southern California.' I got up to pack my bags, and Beau laughed.

'They don't speak French.'

'I speak English!' It's one of the things besides my pictures that I pride myself on. My English is not terrible.

'So do I, but I still don't want to move to the US.'

Closing the door to my studio behind me, I crossed the courtyard with Beau in tow. Though he lived above my studio, he was forever following me into my house.

'Do you think it'll rain?' he asked, peering at the sky.

'I'll ask Auguste. He always knows what the weather will do.' The old winegrower could never give up his work. He must be halfway into his seventies by now, but he was as strong and lively as ever. 'I have to talk to him about the murder anyway.' I pulled on my coat over the scarf I'd not taken off after lunch. 'You coming?'

I didn't have to ask. Thibault would always come along. He couldn't exist without people around to acknowledge his existence, it seemed. But when there was talk of a murder involved, he also wanted to be in the know.

I could live without that curiosity. Also without people. The two together only bred gossip, and like I told *Maman*, I don't listen to gossip.

We strolled along the road in the twilight, down towards my neighbour's house. On my arm was the little basket I always carried when I went to visit him. After his wife died, I got into the habit of bringing him a little something every week. Just a bit of cheese, or a dried sausage, mostly as an excuse to see how he was doing. As it turned out, he was fine and looking forward to teaching his grandson everything he hadn't learned at school, which according to Auguste was almost everything important. But said grandson had only just finished said school and was set on going organic. Needless to say, there had been some altercations in the house of late.

When we approached the kitchen door, we could already hear voices bickering.

'Maybe we should wait?' Beau asked, slowing his step.

I knocked on the door. 'No, this is normal. *Coucou*, Auguste! Brought you some sausage.'

Beau looked sour. I'd taken his sausage. But he'd eaten the one I kept for Auguste.

Once inside the slightly gloomy but large, traditional kitchen, I indicated everyone with my hand. 'Yves, this is my assistant, Thibault. Auguste, you remember Beau. Beau, this is Yves, Auguste's grandson.' I grabbed the sausage to give to Auguste at the exact moment Yves and Beau reached out to shake hands. We ended up all holding the sausage together.

'*Enchanté,*' was Beau's comment.

Yves laughed and let go of the sausage to get a knife. A few years older than Beau, he seemed at least a decade more mature. The first thing you'd notice about him were his vividly blue eyes, which observed the affairs of the world quietly unless they concerned his grandfather. Then, according to the subject, they brimmed with either passion or ice.

'*Papi* and I were just discussing what to have for dinner.'

'No, we were discussing who should prepare it,' Auguste corrected him. 'He's a vegan. He won't eat French food.'

'I eat all kinds of French food. Just nothing that comes from an animal.'

Auguste rolled his eyes and took the knife from his grandson to cut the sausage. Yves winked at us behind Auguste's back.

'So, do you think it'll rain?' Beau asked when he took a seat on the brown leather sofa in a slightly less gloomy living room with dark exposed beams and exhausted furniture from the 1970s. He was probably trying to defuse the situation, but instead made it worse.

'No,' said Auguste, resolutely.

'The forecast says it will,' Yves countered.

'The forecast is wrong.'

Yves opened his mouth, but I was not getting into one of these again.

'I'm afraid I want to ask you about something unpleasant,' I said.

'Did his pesticides kill your plants?' Yves began, but he shrunk back when I glared at him. I'd had some practice with Thibault and was getting seriously good at this.

'It's about the Woman in the Wine.' I addressed Auguste, anxious to see his reaction.

After a quick intake of breath, he frowned and looked between me, Beau, and his grandson with a mix of shock and fear, and I wondered if he'd ever told Yves about what happened. 'Why do you want to know about her?'

'Véronique de Vigan asked me to look into the case.'

'Has she accused anyone?' Auguste asked, and Yves leaned forward.

'No. I asked her if she had any new evidence, but all she said was "not yet". Why she wouldn't simply go to the police if she expected to find evidence somewhere, I don't know, but I'm doing this for a mutual friend.'

Auguste relaxed a little, but his knuckles were white on the armrest of his chair. 'I didn't do it.'

My eyebrows flew up, as did those of Yves and Beau. 'I thought that was obvious from the start?'

'To most, yes. But little girls of six don't always reason the same way adults do. Not even when those girls grow up.' He stared at his knees, lost in thought.

I wondered what Véronique could have said that still got to Auguste after all this time. According to Gilles, she'd only been upset right after it happened and in the last few months, and she'd been abroad most of the years in between. Had she accused Auguste as a six-year-old, or more recently?

'Would you mind telling me what happened? I only spoke to Gilles, but he doesn't want Véronique to delve into the matter, so he wouldn't tell me much.'

'That old *andouille*,' Auguste muttered. He sighed. 'I don't know the whole story either, of course, but I can tell you that Louanne was not happy with him. She called him weak, to put it mildly. I was about the only person in the village who wasn't put off by her take-charge attitude, so she confided in me.'

'You were friends?' I asked.

'Of sorts. Claudine couldn't stand her.' He grinned at Yves, who returned a knowing smile. Whether he'd heard about the rivalry or simply knew how his grandmother could behave, I'd have to ask him later. 'So I couldn't be too obvious about not hating her, but whenever we happened to meet, we'd have a friendly talk that sometimes went deeper. She was never cut

out for village life. Her dreams were bigger. She wanted to sell t
he *caveau* and set up shop in Lyon at least, but Paris if she had
her way.

'To me, though, she had her priorities all wrong. Her first
thoughts should have been for Véronique, but... Well... let's say
she wasn't the motherly type. She saw the *concours culinaire*
as her golden ticket to fame. She would have done anything –
anything – to win that contest. She thought that if she could
claim that prize, the world would be at her feet. I don't know
when she thought that was going to happen, since she'd won
it three times in a row already. And to be honest, her *saucisson
au gène* wasn't even that good. She said it was to the taste
of the judges, who were usually well-known people but often
came from other parts of France, but most of the locals were
convinced she cheated somehow. I believe she would have slept
with the judges if they weren't all women. Never did find out
what kind of power she wielded. And, of course, they shut
down the competition after her death, so I suppose we'll never
know.'

This was all fascinating insight into the dead woman's life.
I made a mental note to check the judges. Times may have
been different, but people weren't. I still didn't know any more
about what happened on the night in question, though.

'Gilles said she'd had quite a bit to drink on the night she
died. Was that a regular occurrence?'

He thought about that. 'She wasn't against drinking. I mean, she owned a wine bar. But I can't remember ever seeing her drunk. Not *that* drunk, anyway.'

'Could she have hidden it well?' Beau asked.

'Seems to me, if you can hide your drunkenness so well that nobody notices, you don't simply keel over into an open wine press,' Yves chimed in.

'Or maybe the fumes from the fermenting grapes...?' I tried, but here Auguste shook his head.

'No, that sort of thing can happen with the open *cuves* used for fermentation, but my *cuvage* is well aired, and that one little stomping vat would not have had such an impact. Even on someone who was already tipsy.'

He would say that, wouldn't he? I'd have to check with an unbiased person. In which case I'd better find out who might have been involved first. If he was right, though, Gilles's accident theory seemed less likely.

'But that means she didn't stumble into the press. Gilles said there was no evidence of a struggle.'

'From what I remember, there were markings, but none of them conclusive.'

'Did the police ever question him? He didn't say, but the husband is usually the most likely suspect.'

Auguste burst out laughing. 'Gilles? The weakest soul in the entire *département du Rhône*? That would almost make me think more of him. What did he do, cuddle her to death? She wouldn't have stood for that.' He wiped the tears from his eyes. 'Of course he was questioned. *Mais allez...* apparently, he was knee deep in laundry when they came to tell him the news, and he broke down crying.'

Auguste's feelings were clear. Gilles was not man enough to kill his wife.

Beau reached for another piece of sausage. 'What was she doing near that press, anyway? How did she get into the winery?'

'Oh, that's easy. I never locked it. Who would want to steal unfinished wine?'

Yves looked shocked. 'Weren't you afraid someone would tamper with the wine?'

Auguste held up his palms. 'Who would want to do that? We may be rival wine growers around here, but we do actually get along quite well, you know.'

'I heard everyone got together to help you out after you weren't able to sell your wine that year,' I said.

Auguste nodded slowly. 'And the next. After that, the quality of my product outweighed the memory of a dead body in my press, and the buyers came back.'

Yves held his hand in the air, and Auguste high-fived him.

'But didn't anyone suspect you?' Beau asked.

'Of course they did!' Auguste was still indignant at the memory. 'All sorts of accusations came flying my way. But through a stroke of luck, Claudine and I had decided to switch up our routine that day. Had she gone to the *viticulteurs* meeting, like she usually did, that would have left me to pick up our son from the train station for the weekend. *I* would have found Louanne, and everyone would have jumped to the conclusion that I had killed her. Instead, it was obvious to everyone that Claudine could not have overpowered Louanne, so something else must have happened. Though nobody ever found out what.'

'It must have been quite a shock to Claudine, finding someone dead in the wine press.'

'She was in therapy for months. Got over it eventually, though. Which is more than can be said for that judge.'

I raised my eyebrows. Finally, something truly new. Could this be the clue I'd been waiting for?

'Oh, right. I keep forgetting you weren't there. You're so much like your mother.'

I smiled. Depending on who said it, I often responded with 'only on the outside', but in this case, I held my tongue. I wanted to know about this judge.

'The competition was judged by three people. Two of them were some sort of celebrity, but one was always the same. Margot Moulin wrote the culinary column for the local newspaper, but she was a well-established name in the industry. Had set up and lost several award-winning restaurants, but she was slowing down, or between fortunes – I can't remember exactly – so she took gigs like judging these kinds of cooking contests. When she heard of Louanne's death, she had a breakdown. I don't know all the details, but from what I heard, she never spoke of the contest again. The police tried to question her, of course, but every time they tried talking about anything to do with the death or the contest, or even mentioned Saint-Maurice, the woman had a fit. Doctors decided she could not be questioned and probably not even trusted if she did say anything about it.'

'That's convenient,' Beau mumbled.

'You would think so. But Margot was in and out of institutions from then on, so her life did not get any better. If she killed Louanne, she was punished for it. If she didn't, that's even sadder, and the killer ruined two lives.'

'If it was a murder and not an accident.' Yves frowned. Throughout Auguste's account, he'd listened attentively, only nodding or shaking his head at certain points.

Falling back in his chair, Auguste waved his hand. 'Only Gilles still clings to that possibility.'

'Well, I'm behind this Véronique. I would want to know who killed my mother too. Absolutely!' Yves turned to his grandfather. 'Did you never want to find out who did it? Clear your name?'

Those blue eyes were on fire. If I played my cards right, maybe Yves could solve this for me. Even easier.

'There was nothing to clear. I was at the meeting the entire evening. Your *mamie* was deemed too weak. Case closed. For us, at least. The whole community had our backs, so we counted ourselves very fortunate.'

'That Margot Moulin sounds suspicious to me,' Beau said, to heavy nodding from Yves.

'But what could possibly be her motive?' I countered. 'She was only there to decide who cooked the best sausage. And the competition hadn't even started. Right?'

Auguste pursed his lips. 'Preparations had been made, of course. The murder happened the day before the contest, but you can't make your *saucisson* on the day. You need at least two days to prepare it and let it cool. I don't think anyone would have let their sausage go to waste, though, when the contest was called off.'

Yves frowned. 'I still think Véronique is right to want to investigate. I'm going to tell her I support her decision.'

While I simpered that *I* would be doing the investigating, Auguste muttered, 'You might want to reconsider. That girl has had it in for me from the beginning.'

Yves didn't seem to notice either of us. He addressed Beau instead. 'Next time you see her, give her my number. I'd be happy to help.'

I cleared my throat and winced in pain. 'Would you mind showing us where the press used to be?' I asked Auguste.

He shrugged, stood, and led the way downstairs to his *cave*, the cellar where he produced his pride and joy, the Beaujolais wine. I'd had the tour long ago, so I knew my way around the *cuves*, the presses, and the little *comptoir* he had set up for tastings. Today, however, I was only interested in the dusty corner behind the wooden barrels that held the ripening wine. Looking at it now, you wouldn't suspect it was once a murder scene. There wasn't even an obvious empty space where the old stomping vat had been. I cast my eye round the walls and ceiling, but nothing stood out.

'Did they find anything at the time?' Beau asked.

Auguste frowned, remembering that awful night. 'I came home from the meeting to find strange cars parked on the drive. The emergency people had left by then. Some police person came out of the house and told me someone had died in my house. I didn't even hear what else he had to say. I ran inside to find my family. Claudine was in shock. Patrick was upset, but talking.'

'Yves's dad,' I explained to Beau.

'Those were my main concerns. Once I'd established that my family was okay, I could finally listen to what had happened. Except nobody knew. Claudine had come home with Patrick and gone down to fetch a bottle. As you can see, the vat was in direct line of sight from the entrance on the other side. Claudine never even went near it, so at first, she didn't know who it was that was hanging over the edge. Patrick came running when she screamed, and he was the one to check if Louanne was still alive. He never said, but I think it was that experience that made him decide not to take over the business.'

Yves clapped a hand on his grandfather's shoulder. 'Good thing I'm here now.'

'You have a lot to learn before I'll allow you to take over.'

'I finished school – I know everything.'

'Ha!' Auguste turned and climbed the stairs. 'That's all I'll say. Ha!'

Bickering once more, they left Beau and me in the *cave*.

'Anything?' Beau asked.

I shrugged with an I-don't-know-what-I'm-supposed-to-find face. 'Not that I can see. But I'm sure it's been thoroughly cleaned several times over in the last thirty years.'

'How big was this thing?'

'The ones I've seen...' I held my hand up about half a metre off the ground. 'And about two metres in diameter. Big enough for two people to get in at once.'

My phone rang and I took the video call. My mother's annoyed face appeared. 'Where are you? I told you I'd be here after work, so why aren't you here?'

Oops. 'Two secs. I'm at Auguste's.'

She hung up without answer.

'Shall we?' Beau grinned.

'We shall.'

7

Another delicious 'fact'

'I'll give you the facts first, so you can decide what to do with them later,' my mother declared after I'd appeased her with a cup of hot chocolate. 'Rumour was' – I loved these kinds of facts – 'that Louanne de Vigan was having an affair with Auguste Prunille.'

That must be one of the accusations that had 'come flying his way'.

'Just a rumour?' Beau asked.

Maman shrugged. 'As far as I know. Louanne was known far and wide to always want a finger in the pie of everything.'

Now, who else did I know that fit that description? I wondered how Louanne had ended up dead, and Apolline had become my mother's hero. Good thing we didn't gossip, or I would tell my mother some 'facts' about Apolline and the way she treated me and everyone else not considered 'her kind of people'.

Thibault scrunched up his face. 'She wanted her finger in an Auguste pie?'

Maman ignored him. 'But her one big thing was the *concours culinaire*. It had been running for over ten years before she got involved, but as soon as she did, she took it over completely. She set the date, she invited the press, she arranged which celebrities would be that year's judges. And of course, she always won.'

'Didn't that make people suspicious?'

She pulled up an eyebrow. 'What do you think? Some people gave up trying, saying it was no use as the cards were marked, so to speak. But others, like Claudine, thought that if they just made outstanding dishes, surely the judges would see their mistake. Claudine was so outspoken in her views that, at first, everyone thought she must have been the one to do away with Louanne, but she couldn't have done it without leaving a trace. And you should have seen her afterwards. There was no way she could have killed her rival, coolly collected her son from the train station, and then sank into such a state of shock at what would have been a fake discovery of the body. Nobody is that good an actress.'

I made a note in my file. 'Okay, so Claudine wasn't strong enough. Auguste has a solid alibi. There must have been more people involved, though?'

Clearing her throat, my mother shifted in her seat. '*Bien sûr.* Trouble was, without evidence of anyone actually having been at the crime scene, the police had only motive to go on, and...

well... that didn't particularly rule out anyone either. The pool of suspects was so large that they didn't know where to begin.'

Beau shook his head. 'That doesn't make sense. There must have been people who were closer to her or who had maybe threatened her. Or what about the other contestants?'

'That's the reasoning the police applied as well. I know they checked out everyone registered for the competition that year. But they never made an arrest.'

'So who were they?' My fingers hovered over the keyboard, ready to list.

'Oh, I don't know.' *Maman* flapped her hand around, and my heart sank. 'It's been so long. Claudine, of course. Lucille Prunille, Auguste's mother. Let's see, who else... There was this little woman, Dina, who moved up north years ago. Oh, and François! He wasn't a very good cook, but he thought participating would help him settle into the village.'

'Settle? Can't be François Simon, then?' The only François I knew was a staple of village life in Saint-Maurice. Every fête, every school event, every council meeting, François was part of it. He was so rooted in the village, I couldn't imagine anything but that his family had been here as long as mine.

But *Maman* nodded excitedly. 'Oh yes, he was new then. Came all the way from Vienne. I think he'd run from a lost love or something, but that's only hearsay.'

Another delicious 'fact'.

'What about the judges?' Beau inquired. 'Especially that one that never had to talk about the murder.'

'Ah, yes.' My mother took a deep breath, probably sorting facts from gossip in her head. Though we did not do gossip, one picks up things, you know? 'There were only two judges that year. The third had called in sick at the last moment. You can imagine how Louanne felt about that. I'm sure I wasn't surprised when I heard she'd been drinking. Her perfect competition would be less than perfect! Anyway, one judge was the same as always – Margot Moulin. That's the one you were talking about.' She inclined her head towards Beau. 'The other was Renate Reinhart, from Alsace. She sang that song about *viennoiseries*, you know?' She hummed a tune that I recognised but couldn't put words to. 'She was quasi famous for a while in the late eighties. No idea what she's up to these days.'

I stared at my list of suspects. Claudine, passed away. Auguste's mother, long dead. Unknown little woman, might as well be dead. Once-famous singer... I supposed I could look into her, but what could possibly have motivated her to kill a nobody in a town she didn't know? Same went for the other judge, of course, Margot Moulin. But at least she was supposed to be local, so I'd look her up.

And François. I liked him. And he loved to talk, so I'd pay him a visit in the morning. Maybe he would remember things differently since he didn't know people very well at the time.

Imagine that! François, not knowing anyone! I unconsciously shook my head.

Maman took it as something else. 'I don't think Renate had anything to do with it either. She was whisked away by her agent at the first whiff of negative publicity. But Margot was an odd one. She only ever dealt with Louanne and always stayed in the same room at the hotel.'

'What, our hotel? The one that Jeanette Ta is doing up?'

'At the time, it had a more than sufficient client base. It was the heyday of the Beaujolais Nouveau.' As the mayor of Saint-Maurice, my mother had to encourage every new commercial attempt, but privately, she wasn't convinced Saint-Maurice would attract the necessary clientèle to keep a hotel running. She'd warned me of this before I invested, but I couldn't help myself. Not all the rooms might be full all nights, but Théo's cooking would fill the restaurant every day. And this was my friend's dream! What better use for my money?

'I still think it's suspicious that she couldn't talk about the murder afterwards. That's as good as an admission of guilt,' Beau said.

'A lot of people thought that at the time. But nobody could come up with a good motive. And in the end, if she had done it, she'd more or less punished herself for it. That was enough for most.'

'Is that what you think happened?' I asked my mother.

'I was never convinced one way or the other. Of course, your grandfather was mayor at the time, and I was about to become part of the family. Although, on that day... I mean... oh, *peu importe*. Even if I'd had an opinion on the matter, I wouldn't have voiced it without evidence. But because there was no evidence, I didn't have an opinion.'

Very politically correct. My brother David would no doubt agree. 'No idea at all?'

'If I had, I would have acted on it. In the name of justice,' she added pointedly. Then she sighed. 'I don't know how you get yourself mixed up in these things. There's nothing to gain.'

Beau showed a wicked grin. ''Cause she's a smitten kitten.'

My mother's eyes widened and I felt my cheeks grow so hot I was sure I'd become radioactive.

'She's got the hots for a cactus.' Thibault continued his torture.

'A cactus?' Her brow furrowed.

'I'm not. I don't. He's not... He's...' I swallowed, wincing. 'I'm doing it for a friend.'

'What friend?'

I should have seen that one coming. 'Léon?' Since everything I'd remembered about him before was wrong, I wasn't sure if I ever told my mother about him.

'Oh!' The sun broke through on my mother's face. I must have told her before he fell from grace in my memory. 'I did wonder whatever happened to him. But it never felt like the right moment to ask.'

Meaning, tell me all! But I wasn't going to. Maybe one day.

I wish Beau had picked up on that sentiment. 'He's with Véronique now. And together they steamrolled Julie into investigating. It was a thing of beauty.' He gave a chef's kiss to show his appreciation, but I had a different opinion on what had happened.

'*She* asked me, and he said he didn't agree.'

'Yes! He went for the total emotional blackmail.' He twisted his voice and posture to imitate Léon's. 'But if you're set on being brilliant for us, we won't stand in your way.'

It was an eerily good impression, but I wasn't laughing. Was that really what had happened? Had I been played by someone I thought was a friend? My insecurities about Léon washed over me, and I clasped my hands together to keep them from shaking.

Frowning, Beau narrowed his eyes at me. 'You know, the way you were talking about him, I expected more.'

'What do you mean, *more*?' My clasped hands balled to fists. What more could anyone expect than what Léon had? And just like that, my doubts and fears were gone. Léon would never play me! How dare Thibault suggest such a thing.

'Well, you know... more handsome, *quoi*. This guy is so... ordinary.'

'I thought you liked him.' I could barely keep from shouting. My mother noticed and laid a hand on my knee.

'I do, actually,' an oblivious Beau chuckled.

'Not everyone needs that superficial beauty that you have. His comes out when he smiles and when he speaks.'

Now his smile faded. His hurt eyes met mine, and he blinked. 'I'm sorry,' he said simply.

'I didn't mean all you have is outward beauty,' I conceded.

'Hooray, we're all friends again!' My mother threw her hands up, drenching herself with the last forgotten sips of chocolate. My laugh turned into a painful cough in an instant punishment for my schadenfreude.

8
You should probably start knitting or something

Three Decades earlier

'I've been waiting ten minutes. I said I'd be here. Why weren't you?'

Flora inwardly rolled her eyes. 'I'm sorry, *Maman*. I had to take some of the volunteers to Villefranche.'

Her mother huffed. 'I wish you'd called.'

'Finding a pay phone would have just made me even later.'

Her mother murmured on for a while, but Flora didn't listen. Since the moment she left Nicolas's flat, one person after another had kept her busy with this thing or that. Though she loved helping people out, today her heart wasn't in it. She badly needed some time alone to think. To consider her future. What would a future with Nicolas look like? And could there even be one without him?

'*Coucou!*' Her mother's hand waved in front of Flora's eyes. 'Did you hear what I said?'

Trying to remember her mother's last words, Flora blinked. Nothing came up.

'What's wrong, *ma belle*?' Suddenly, her mother's tone was quite different. Concern in her eyes, she laid a soft hand on Flora's cheek.

Did she want to talk about it? She shook her head. 'Nothing. Just stuff I need to think about.'

'Does this stuff have anything to do with the fact that Nicolas isn't here?'

Mothers! How did they always know?

'Couples fight, *chérie*. As long as it doesn't happen too often, there's nothing wrong with that.'

'We didn't fight.' Flora wished her mother would stop digging. She just wanted to be alone.

'Okay... Well, we'd better get a move on if we want to be on time.'

Flora gave her mother a blank look.

'We're supposed to be at the prize reveal in ten minutes. You do want to be there? It's Nicolas's big moment.'

No, it wasn't. His big moment had been this morning, and she'd ruined it. How could she now go stand in the crowd and cheer him on? But not going would also look weird. Everyone would expect her to be there.

Ugh! See? The expectations were already limiting her, and they weren't even married! She would refuse to go. That would show everyone.

'All right, let's go.' Maybe she could grow a backbone before the next time. But if she was honest with herself, she was also a tiny bit curious to see how Nicolas had taken her running off. Would he be devastated? Have red eyes? Slumped shoulders?

Anything but smiling and joking with everyone as if nothing had happened! Her eyes had searched the crowd as soon as they'd approached the square. At least half the village must be there. But she'd spotted his almost black, wavy hair near the podium, where he would be revealing the grand prize for the *concours culinaire* in about ten minutes. Surrounded by either sour or benevolent-looking members of his family, he chatted with the judges and some of the village's more prominent people, showing that carefree smile Flora loved so much.

But how could he be showing it now? She'd ignored his offer of marriage. Had she not crushed his world? How could he be this cheerful when her own life was upside down?

'Come on, *mon bonbon*.' Her mother pulled her along, as Flora appeared to have stopped walking after seeing Nicolas. She made sure not to advance too far into the crowd, holding her mother back. As her mother was one to always be front and centre, this obviously displeased her, but she was sensitive enough to her daughter's feelings to adhere to her wishes.

Her mother had been ecstatic about her relationship with Nico from the start. She liked him, but mostly she'd seen the possibilities for Flora.

'You'd be wonderful in that position.' 'You could do so much good for the village.' 'It would be perfect for you.' Not him. It. As if she'd applied for a job. Perhaps she could blame her mother for not wanting the job now that it was actually offered.

Because that's what it felt like. Nicolas would be horrified to know that's how she saw his proposal. He loved her. He just wanted to be with her forever. And isn't that what she wanted? But not if it came with all these extras. Having to stand there, on that podium, in between all the other notables – mostly his family – and smile and wave and encourage everyone to do their best... She shuddered.

Claudine Prunille hurried past on her way to the podium.

'Come on, Claudine! I'm rooting for you!' Flora shouted at her back. She was rewarded with a nervous smile over a shoulder.

'Hey, what about me?' François put on an indignant face as he followed Claudine, and Flora grinned.

'You get to enjoy your own cooking afterwards. That should be reward enough.'

The Family had mounted the steps to the little podium and now looked sour and benevolent down their noses. How Flora had found grace with all of them was still a mystery to her. Nico's father, the mayor, who was now addressing the crowd, was like a cunning teddy bear. He was so sweet, you just felt like cuddling him all the time. This quality had fooled people into thinking they could pull a fast one on him, but he'd cheated them instead. All for the good of the village, naturally. After all, the teddy bear part was real.

This suited Nico's mother very well. Lana was not a hugger. She was the efficient woman behind the man, making sure the home was well organised and the decisions about the village her husband made were well executed. She could be a little distant but had a kind heart and was an inspiration to Flora. How would she react to the news of Flora's not-yet-refusal? How would either of them react? Did they already know?

Suddenly it seemed all the members of the Family were scanning the crowd like RoboCops. Flora flapped the front panels of her denim jacket to cool down but couldn't shake the feeling of being watched and judged. For the second time that day, she fled the scene.

Getting away from curious eyes isn't easy in a village where everybody knows each other. Pushing through the growing crowd, she thought about slipping into the church, but surely someone would notice and start a serious rumour. She ducked around the corner, rounded one of the buttresses, and sagged against the church wall, closing her eyes. This was ridiculous. She couldn't keep hiding forever. Running away wasn't going to change her situation. But she desperately needed time to be alone and think. To consider whether she loved Nicolas enough to marry an entire village.

'Undignified, isn't it? I think the whole thing is in poor taste. Not that anyone ever listens to me.'

Flora didn't have to open her eyes to know that the person speaking was Nico's Aunt Géraldine. No doubt smoking a cigarette.

'They all seem to like it.'

'It's food. We're French.' As an explanation for the crowd, that would do. But it didn't tell Flora why Géraldine was hiding from the ceremony. But then, she was always the odd one out. In her manner and beliefs, she was as old-fashioned as they came, still clinging to the feudal system that had been abolished with the French Revolution. Only old money was real money, in her opinion. She'd never married because life was better alone than shared with someone sub-par. But she had seen more of the world than all the rest combined, travelling to far-away places where they didn't even speak French.

Flora opened her eyes to see if that would coax more out of her unexpected companion.

'Look, I'll tell you what I told Lana. You'll have to learn to pick your moments. *Noblesse oblige*, but when there's yet another *nouveau riche* wanting to dig one of those tawdry swimming pools in their garden, you'll need to know when to take a moment to yourself before you tell them in no uncertain terms what you think of them. Lana goes to see an opera. I travel. You' – she sighed, regarding Flora with a strange mix of pity and warmth – 'should probably start knitting or something.'

Was that an insult? It felt like an insult. But almost everything Géraldine said felt like an insult, even if she wasn't talking to you or about you. This was probably her version of motherly advice.

'Thank you.'

Géraldine smiled. 'I think you'll do well with Nico. He's a bit of a privateer – in service of the people, but in his own scallywag way. He'll keep you from being too nice, and you'll keep him on the right track.'

Odd, to hear someone 'in service of the people' encourage her love, while her own mother had encouraged her career as a wife. It made Flora extra grateful for Géraldine's words, and she gave her a genuine smile. Flora would have gone for a hug, but that would not have been appreciated.

Still, would love be enough to support her 'career'?

Géraldine gave her a rare hand squeeze before returning to her post. Flora stayed behind, not sure if what Géraldine had said made her more determined to go for it, or to call it quits. In one case, she'd be stuck in the village. In the other, she'd have to move away and never return.

Flora didn't like opera. She preferred musicals. Could they be her temporary escape? She could always take up knitting. She groaned, pushing her palms to her eyes. Better get back to her mother. She'd find some time to think later.

She returned to the square to thunderous applause. Nicolas must have revealed the tropical holiday that was this year's prize. He'd been so excited to tell her about how he found this amazing little beach hut with every amenity close by, but still far enough away from the tourist crowds to enjoy the quiet of the ocean. Though Flora had no desire to travel, the way he'd spoken about it had made her long to be there. She grinned, seeing his enthusiasm in the light of Géraldine's moniker for him. A privateer fit exactly on the white, sandy beach he'd described.

A hollow feeling sank to the pit of her stomach. She did love him, and he loved her. She'd known this moment would come. But she'd put off thinking about it, seeing a proposal as something for the future. Now that it was here, it was so much scarier than she'd anticipated. Couldn't he have picked a moment with less pressure? The cooking contest was an even bigger affair than the Beaujolais Nouveau celebrations for the community of Saint-Maurice. Could she be up there with the cuddly mayor, his composed wife, and his carefree son? She was a nervous mess even down here in the crowd.

One last round of applause announced the end of the assemblage. The Family descended and the crowd dispersed. Nicolas remained up there with Renate Reinhart. With her bright pink eye make-up and crimped hair, leg warmers layered over leggings and ankle boots, a denim shirt tied around her hips, she was at the peak of fashion. She looked like someone who should be on a podium. The way she was flirting with Nicolas, she could be the next in line if Flora wasn't careful.

There shouldn't *be* a next in line! Driven by jealousy, Flora stomped up the few steps to the podium.

'*Ah, coucou, chérie,*' Nicolas said with a smile, holding his hand out towards her. As if nothing had happened, he introduced her to the pretty singer, but then he added, 'My fiancée.'

Only because the disappointed look on Renate's face was worth it, Flora didn't comment. Too bad for her, this one was taken. Maybe.

But Renate recovered quickly. She went on and on about how she knew nothing about cooking, but that this was a fantastic opportunity and how she would use it to build her career. Nicolas kept her going, but all the while, Flora was distractingly aware of his arm around her waist. She shouldn't have come up here. They were in full view of everyone in the middle of the village square. The fact that nobody actually seemed interested was beside the point. He had proposed, and she had not said yes, and this situation was far too mundane to follow that. How come *she* was an emotional mess, and *he* got to stand here and smile at a pretty girl?

After a long tennis match of hitting compliments to and fro, Renate finally lobbed them a happy 'See you tomorrow' and left the stage.

Nicolas tugged Flora to his chest and leaned in to kiss her, but she dodged his lips.

'What's wrong?'

Why are you not taking me seriously? 'Can we get down from here? I feel like we're on display.'

He grinned. 'So? It's not like we're a secret.' But he released her nonetheless, and she dashed down the steps, once more looking for a quiet corner. The alley next to the hotel led to a narrow street flanked only on one side by a row of houses. A low wall on the other side lined a field that had gone fallow since the owner died a few years before. Nico's dad had wanted to get his hands on it for some time, but right then, it was as calm a spot as Flora was going to find close by.

'So now I'm your fiancée?' she asked as soon as she felt more private, not managing to keep a slight note of hysteria out of her tone.

He shrugged. 'It's only a matter of time, right?'

'You can't assume, just because I didn't say no, that the answer will automatically be yes!'

'Well... what else is there?'

'It might still be no.' The chances of that were growing by the minute. How did he not realise this was a major issue for her?

'But... you love me.'

She almost rolled her eyes. 'There's a lot more to marriage than love. Especially a marriage to you.'

His eyebrows shot up, and he held up his palms. 'What's so special about me?'

That knocked the wind out of her sails for a moment. It would have been adorable if she wasn't so upset with his ignorance.

'Nico—'

'Ah, there you are.'

Flora groaned. Louanne was the last person she wanted to talk to right now. But Nicolas had already extended a jovial greeting.

'Yes, hi. I want you two to talk to the contestants. See what they think of the prize and such. I'll write up an article for that *Courant* person to print.'

Playing innocent, Nicolas smiled. 'All right, Louanne. What do you think of the prize, and who are you going to enjoy it with if you win?'

'Not me!' Louanne spat. 'I'm writing the piece. I can make up my own entry. Have a word with the others before they all go home. I spent too long dealing with that Moulin woman already. Off you go, *allez*!'

She grabbed them both by the shoulder like a couple of naughty teenagers and shoved them in the direction of the hotel. This was intolerable. Flora would let her know she did not wish to be treated that way. She would mince no words. She would stand up to that bully. As soon as the interviews were over.

9

How have you been?

My head felt too heavy to lift the next morning, so I didn't. I had been a good little Juju last night and gone to bed ridiculously early. The fact that I'd instantly fallen asleep said enough about my condition. But now that I was awake, it hit me even harder. My lungs rasped, my throat was twice its normal size, and my head was leaden.

Luckily, I didn't have any clients today. The only thing on my agenda was looking into a thirty-year-old murder. Well, the woman had been dead for so long, she could wait another day. Besides, it was still dark, so probably the middle of the night.

My phone pinged with a message. Though I'd rather keep my eyes closed, I checked my smartwatch anyway. Not that I was curious, but it might be important, you see?

Mind if I come over?

In the middle of the night? My watch said 8:30. Oh, right, winter. Now that my eyes were open, I could see it wasn't actually as dark as I'd thought. I sighed.

Of course not :)

That message was happier than me.

Good, cos I'm on my way :)

WHAT?! Panic mode! How dare he add a smiley face to that harrowing message. I jumped out of bed, piling on jumpers as I found them, hoisting myself into some tights, and zipping up a skirt just as the doorbell rang. My face! I cracked open the window and called down, 'Just a minute!' Or two. Or three. Contacts. Mascara. Lipstick. A very costume-drama pinch to my cheeks would have to do. I ran out of the bathroom and back in. Breath mint.

I made it to the front door wheezing and puffing like an ancient vacuum cleaner. Deep breath. Hold it in. Coughing fit.

'Are you okay?' Léon asked through the closed door.

'*Ouaaai,*' I hissed. Out of excuses, I opened the door with tears in my eyes to reveal a concerned-looking Léon.

'You don't look okay.'

I groaned. Thanks.

He took me by the arm and led me to the kitchen, carefully closing the door behind him. 'I think you should leave the sleuthing till later. Did I wake you?'

Was it that obvious? 'No, of course not. Early riser, me. Get my best work done in the morning.' I wished I hadn't said anything. Every word hurt my throat, my lungs, and my head.

'That's different from before, then,' he said with a smile that conveyed how much he didn't believe me.

I pulled up the corner of my mouth in a half-hearted attempt at a smile.

He filled the kettle and turned, leaning against the counter. 'I think you're amazing, getting to where you are now from where you were.'

After the few seconds it took for his unexpected words to sink in, I felt myself sit up a little straighter. You know what? My head didn't hurt so much after all.

'How have you been?'

He wasn't asking about yesterday. He knew me too well. He really wanted to know. And for the first time since I'd escaped my ex-husband, I wanted to tell. In the safety of my kitchen, with my friend right there, I could finally let my mind open up to the horrors I'd been through with Franck's abuse, the divorce, his fraud, his conviction, his death threat, and finally, my very slow but eventual climb out of that pit.

I wanted to tell, but all I said was 'Miserable.' I managed a watery smile and wiped away a wayward tear. 'But better now.'

He nodded, not pushing for anything more. 'I hope we can stay in touch this time.'

My smile grew a little bigger. 'I'd like that.'

We stared at each other in silence until the kettle clicked off.

'Water's done,' I said, not taking my eyes off him. How could Beau say this man was ordinary? Sure, his hair was thinning a bit, and you wouldn't look to him for bulging muscles, but look at those eyes. That smile! When he looked at me, he really saw me. No need for lies or embellishments. If only I'd met him before Franck.

But then, maybe I wouldn't have been interested. After my father died, Franck had reminded me of all the great things about Dad – the cheeky jokes, the confidence, the intelligence. He was the kind of man I wanted at the time. Léon would have paled in comparison. But I'd closed my eyes to the ruthlessness. Didn't see that Franck lacked the love my dad had in abundance.

By the time I met Léon, that had become painfully obvious. Franck only wanted a yes-girl, someone to admire and adore him and only him. Someone who would devote her life to him and not have any needs of her own. When I turned out not to be this soulless character, he bombarded me with sighs and complaints about what a disappointment I was. And I was foolish enough to believe him. Until I met Léon.

I tore my gaze away from this extraordinary man and offered him coffee. He accepted and took a seat at the kitchen table.

'So how have *you* been?' I asked while filling the cafetière.

He breathed in through his nose. 'After the trial, I took a teaching job in the States. I told you I'd been interested in going there for a while, but I'd put it off.'

My eyes widened. 'Because of me?' I couldn't bear it if that were true. If he'd put his life on hold for me and I'd shut him out of mine.

He gave a half-smile. 'Well... partly, maybe. But my mother wasn't well at the time, so I wanted to be there for her too.'

Now that he mentioned it, I remembered him telling me about that. I should probably have inquired after her. Why am I so self-absorbed? 'How is your mother now?'

'Oh, she's fine. She and Dad are going on a cruise in a few months. She's been nagging me that we'll have too little time together beforehand. I only got back here a few weeks ago, *tu vois*. Now that Véronique's here, too, she says she doesn't see me enough.'

'Did you meet her in America?' What did I care about Véronique? Nothing, that's what. But now he'd brought her up, it would be rude not to ask about her. I filled a mug with coffee, turned, and sneezed. Into the coffee.

'I'll have that one, if you don't mind.' Cool as a cucumber. Not one laugh at my faux pas. Just a matter-of-fact request.

My cheeks radiated, and I quickly turned to fill the other mug.

'It was a chance meeting,' Léon continued behind me. 'She was a guest lecturer at my university, and we got talking because we're both French. Then when it turned out that we were both from the same region, we had enough in common to talk about over a few more dates. By then we'd found more common ground, so we've been together – well, apart together because we've lived in different states throughout – for about a year. Now that my contract ended, she suddenly declared she'd been thinking about coming back to France, and here we are.'

'Still apart together?' Not that I was curious. The words just came out. I slid the coffee mug onto the table, careful to keep if away from my breath.

Léon took a sip, then held up his finger to pause the conversation and stalked out of the kitchen. I heard the front door, then a car door, the front door again, and Léon returned with a paper bag from the bakery in the village. Three normal croissants tumbled out, followed by one almond croissant. This man. He'd remembered.

He dipped his croissant in his coffee, while I eyed the candy croissant.

'That's yours, of course,' he said after swallowing, pushing the deliciousness towards me. He didn't have to tell me twice. Bad breakfast choices? An almond croissant is never a bad choice. Especially one that Celine has made.

'Julie, can I have a day off?' Thibault burst into the room, his hair a mess and his shirt unbuttoned.

I blinked at this uncharacteristic behaviour. Not the bursting – he did that regularly. But he always made sure he looked his best. 'Yes, Beau. You're not in an office, and I don't want to use that complicated double system of accumulating days off before you can use them. Please, take a day off!'

'Merci.' He was already out the door again.

With a scrunched-up brow, Léon pointed his thumb at the door. 'You and Beau...?'

I put on my most horrified face, though this question came up a lot. 'No! He's more like my pet assistant.'

He grinned. Good. He'd better not get the wrong impression. I was free as a bird. Whatever not answering my question about them being apart together meant, if there was any chance Véronique would be stupid enough to give this man up, he should know he could cry on my shoulder. And the little voice telling me I had no right to think that could go cook herself an egg.

'I hope you haven't agreed to look into Véronique's case out of politeness. You must be very busy.'

I shrugged. 'It's winter' was the only explanation I was willing to give. 'I can ask around.' I wasn't going to let an insignificant little cold virus keep me from seeing more of Léon, even if he only acted as a middleman. Of course, that contempt for the bug in my body resulted in a nice coughing fit.

'Are you sure you shouldn't be in bed?'

I shook my head, then clutched it.

'How about some aspirin at least?'

That was probably a good idea. I went up to the bathroom to get some and took the opportunity to apply a bit more character to my face. When I returned, Léon had a kind of bashful look on his face.

'I hope you don't consider this forward, but if you wanted to do your asking around today, maybe I could come with you? Two heads are better than one, and since Thibault is off...'

Spend more time with you? Yes, please! 'You don't have to do that.' Hang my polite upbringing!

'I'd like to. I feel bad about asking you to investigate when you're clearly not well. And besides, it'll give us a chance to catch up.'

Who could resist that smile? 'I do have an appointment with the contractor for the hotel at eleven. I was going to go see François before then, but first I have to see if I can find Margot Moulin and make an appointment.'

'All right.' He took out his phone and starting tapping. 'Who are they? Ah, I see Margot Moulin is a former restaurateur. Why are we talking to her?'

While I made myself some herbal tea with honey, I brought Léon up to speed on what we'd found out. He nodded while I talked but stared at the table when I finished.

'I agree with Gilles. It's unhealthy, the way she's obsessed with finding out what happened to her mother. She never mentioned it until I said I was going back to Villefranche. Then suddenly, out comes the story of her mother's murder and how she's never been able to let it go. It's been a constant obstacle between us since that moment. I want to help her, but not in the way she wants to be helped. Do you think it's at all possible you'll find something new, or should she just let it go?'

I hate moral struggles. Why can't I just say, 'Yes, she should let it go, and I should be in bed'? Why do I have to be all, 'We're talking about her mother. If you were her, wouldn't you want to know what happened?'

'Of course. That's what I thought too, at first. But she never mentioned it before, and now it's all she can talk about. Once, she even said she thought her mother was killed because of some treasure. She's becoming some sort of very niche conspiracy theorist.'

'Where did she get the treasure idea?' No one else had mentioned that.

He threw his hand in the air. 'I don't know. She was a bit tipsy at the time and she never mentioned it again, but when she said it, she sounded serious enough for me to change my mind about being supportive of her goals. She was going too far. As soon as Gilles talked about the recent goings-on in the village and your involvement in them, she was determined we search you out and ask you to get involved. I tried to dissuade her, but in the end... I'm afraid I selfishly saw it as an opportunity to get back in touch.'

'I'm glad you did.' A genuine spark of gratefulness towards Véronique surprised me. Maybe I wasn't doomed after all. Time to put this positive energy into action and make good on my promise. I nodded at his phone. 'What else does it say about Margot Moulin?'

10

I know what you're here for

We spent half an hour researching Margot Moulin and planning our day. My painkiller kicked in, and I felt optimistic that together with Léon, I would uncover something. It might not lead us to a killer, but at least I'd have something to show Véronique. I'd also decided that if Léon loved her, I should think more positively about her. What if they got married? I'd still want him as my friend, so I should try to get along with her too.

In that mindset, I was chatting to my friend about all my plans for the business as we left to talk to François. He seemed a bit distracted, but then I noticed Anne-Bonny, my new neighbour, talking to her phone on a selfie-stick, twirling her pink hair with a flourish. When she spotted us, she lowered the phone and hobbled towards us on shiny blue platform boots.

'Julie! I can't believe I didn't recognise you last time. You're, like, one of my heroes. I don't know if you've seen my feed, but I copy so many of your poses and people always love them. Next time, I'll tag you. For free, of course! My agent hates when I do that, but he gets paid enough.' She tinkled a laugh, then shivered. No wonder – it was the beginning of January and she wore nothing but some sort of bikini, covered with a loose, off-the-shoulder top and a fuchsia tutu.

'Thank you. I'm honoured.' I think? I would have to check out her social media to see if her influence would actually help my business, but it couldn't hurt. 'You look cold. I think you'd better go back inside.'

'Oh, don't worry about me. I get hurt doing stupid stuff all the time. It's kinda my trademark. People expect it. And I don't even do it on purpose. Talk about living your brand, *non*?' She laughed out loud but retreated into the warmth of her new house nonetheless.

Léon blinked a few times. 'Interesting girl.'

I grinned. 'Her name's Anne-Bonny. Apparently, she's an influencer, but I've yet to check out her stuff.' I sneeze-coughed, feeling dizzy with the force of it, but Léon's pitying look only made me more determined to press on. 'François is usually at the *bar-tabac* in the morning.' Jeanette's café doubled as a social gathering spot in so many ways that I sometimes wondered what would happen to the village dynamics after she opened the hotel and closed the little *bar-tabac*.

'*Bonjour,*' I called out to the community inside. Several *bonjours* echoed back to me, but more pairs of eyes rested on my unknown companion. I scanned the room for François but found Isabelle Cochon, the butcher's wife, instead. She was talking to Bella Dudevant, whom I didn't want to call my arch-nemesis because I didn't want her to be that important. But let's just say she had done plenty to annoy me.

Isabelle had her most knowing face on. She fished a lighter out of her pocket with her thumb and pinkie, a gesture practised over years of holding a cigarette between her other fingers, and continued her gossip about someone or other. 'She has no self-control. She says people aren't used to women having a PhD yet because they say to her, "*You* have a PhD?" But it's just her. They can't believe *she* would be smart enough.'

Bella shrugged. 'I don't know. I'm pretty smart myself, but don't expect me to perform any mathematical equations.'

'No?' I heard myself asking. Why did I do that? I didn't want to talk to her. It was only that petty little part of me that wanted to hear more about something she could not do. I hated that part. I wished it would keep its mouth shut. 'No good at maths?'

She cackled. 'That's not it. If I wanted to work out the value of X, I would have done it before he became an ex.'

Both she and the butcher's wife burst out laughing, and I hung my head. Served me right. 'I'm looking for François. Have you seen him?'

Bella pointed her chin to the right, which I took as my cue to leave. She cast Léon an uninterested look, then continued her conversation. Showed what she knew. Thibault she was all over. The beauty that was Léon she couldn't care less about. Her loss.

I led Léon to the counter, where François presided.

'Ah! The girl of the hour. I know what you're here for,' he said, beaming. 'You want to hear the story of the Woman in the Wine.'

'How did you...' But I knew the answer before I'd finished the question.

'Isabelle, of course,' François said, his jolly jowls quivering on either side of his grey walrus moustache. 'Well, you've come to the right place. It may be over thirty years ago, but that doesn't mean I don't remember it like it was yesterday.'

I pulled up a barstool for Léon and myself since François had already launched into his story.

'We had just moved from Vienne,' he explained to Léon, 'It was just my wife and I – our children hadn't been born yet, and I wanted to get to know the people in the village. What better way than to enter in the *concours culinaire* that was such a big deal around these parts? Hmmm... You know what they say, be careful what you wish for. I got to know them all right. I was' – he counted on his fingers – 'an outsider, a bad cook, a *man*.' Here he gently placed his fingertips at the base of his throat and cast his gaze heavenwards. 'And rude. Most of these labels came from Louanne de Vigan, the self-proclaimed *reine du concours*. But even the queen couldn't stop me from entering the contest. She also couldn't stop me from having fun with it. Because she was right, *tu sais*? I was all those things she said, except rude. The rude bit was that I didn't drop out of the competition at her wish since I was having too much fun.'

'How did you hear about the contest anyway?' I asked.

'From Cédric Roche. Do you know him?'

I nodded. Cédric was an old friend of my mother's.

'This was before the distillery closed, obviously. They made the most marvellous Marc de Bourgogne.' François smacked his lips, remembering the taste of the liquor, but Léon threw me an uncertain look.

'A *gnôle*,' François explained without result. 'A *goutte*? *Eau-de-vie?*'

Finally, the penny dropped.

'There you go. Now that was a real man's drink. Such a shame they stopped producing. I go to Pruniers now. They also have a good brandy, but not as smooth as the Saint-Maurice one.'

'François, the competition?' This could go on forever in various directions and on numerous tangents. I had to try and guide the narrative.

'Yes, yes, I'll get to that. *T'inquiète pas.* What was I talking about? Ah, right, Cédric. He worked at the distillery, so he also had ties with the vineyard owners and the cooking contest.'

I followed his logic in my head. The local brandy was distilled from the same *marc de raisin,* the grape skins left over after pressing, that was used in the recipe for the sauce that accompanied the *saucisson au gène,* the local delicacy that was the focus of the *concours culinaire.* In wine country, everything is connected to grapes in one way or another.

'Seeing how much I appreciated the local delicacies, he suggested I enter the contest as well. Nobody would mind if my dish wasn't up to standard. He was right at that. All the ladies came to my rescue because they pitied my terrible cooking.' He bellowed out a laugh. 'If I'd had any talent at all, my dish would have won after all their tips and tricks. But I believe my embonpoint started then and there.' He rubbed his sizeable belly and took a sip of his coffee.

The painkiller I'd taken earlier was starting to wear off. I wished François would get to the point.

'What do you think happened on the night of Louanne de Vigan's death?' Léon's serious words sobered François somewhat.

He blinked a few times, then continued his story in a more sedate tone. 'The day before the contest, we'd been preparing our sausages under the watchful eye of the judges. Though I wasn't seriously competing, I got swept up in the drama and didn't want to lose face, so I'd concentrated just as much as the others. By five o'clock, when the buzzer sounded the end of the first leg of the competition, the excitement of the day had us all ready for a drink.

'They rushed us off to the square, where your dad told us of the wonderful holiday I was never going to win, and back to the hotel for an interview. I don't even remember who the interviewer was or what it was about, but you can imagine that when we were done, that drink looked a lot more attractive than dinner. Who needs more food after cooking and tasting all day? But the drink hit all the harder.' He rotated his fist in front of his nose to indicate the extent of drunkenness.

'That evening, even Louanne was friendly. But then, she had enjoyed quite a few. Must have been extra stressful for her, making sure the event went smoothly but also cooking with the intent to win. Still, she joined us in the *caveau* for a glass or two. We were all pretty merry after a few hours, but she was *bourrée*. When I heard Gilles had let her go out by herself that night, I couldn't believe it. But at the time, I chalked it up to the difference between the big city and the countryside. What could happen, *quoi*?' He spread out his arms, palms up, and paused to take a sip of coffee.

'We were all in shock. Of the locals, Claudine took it hardest, probably because she found the body. But Margot

Moulin took it even worse, even though I don't think she liked Louanne much. She always preferred talking to the other candidates, which... you know... who can blame her? We had loads of laughs, Margot and I. Went to visit her at the clinic, too, afterwards. She must have had a good day because we reminisced about all the fun stuff that happened. Even years later, she knew exactly who I was. Wonderful woman. But she never spoke of that night again.'

Taking another sip of coffee, François switched subjects, the sparkle back in his eyes. 'I saw you in the *caveau* last week, with Tiana and the American, sitting by that silly painting. Did you know that was the first thing Gilles changed when he inherited the *caveau*? Used to be some sort of glass artwork of grapes or something. Everything around here is grapes. Grapes, grapes, grapes. I wonder if—'

'Do you remember anything else about that night?'

Annoyed that Léon wouldn't let him finish his prattle, François's eyes darkened. 'You're wasting your time, *mon gars*. If I or anyone that was there had known anything, we would have said so at the time. But we didn't know then, and we know even less now. It's an anecdote, let it be.'

He turned demonstratively away from us, dismissing us like bothersome paparazzi. I was about to press him further when Madame Dufaux tapped my shoulder.

'Julie, it's my husband's birthday next month, and I thought... *Tiens*... I mean, he puts the cracked egg shells back into the carton with the whole ones, but he's a good man, really. And... well, Isabelle said...'

Where was she going with this? My headache was back with a vengeance.

'You're a pin-up photographer and all, so... Would I have to bring my own feathers and lace?'

I choked, shaking my head equally at her and at Léon, who mercifully showed no signs of discomfort. 'No! No, it's not that kind of pin-up. Just frilly pants. Also, lots of teasing, curling, and false lashes. But no feathers. No lace. If you want that kind of picture, you'll have to find somebody el se.'

Madame Dufaux looked confused but then broke into a slow smile. 'Frilly pants? Interesting.' She floated away on a cloud of thoughts I didn't want to know.

I turned back to François, but he was now laughing at something the woman on his other side had said, and I doubted he would tell us anything more, even if he did know something. Perhaps I could corner him somewhere more private later and ask again, but for now, we'd heard everything we were going to hear.

As we exited the café, we encountered Isabelle in a cloud of cigarette smoke.

'Thank you for recommending me,' I began. 'But I'm not that kind of photographer. Please get your facts— Wait. I thought you'd quit smoking?'

Isabelle grunted at me. 'Look, I know you're new. New again. You know what I mean. You've been gone for so long, you're practically an outsider now. So I'll forgive you for not knowing. It's the new year. Everyone knows that I make a New Year's resolution to quit smoking, but by the Fête des Rois, I've given up. That's just the way it is.'

Six days. Epiphany would be the day after tomorrow, so she hadn't even made it four days. Some resolution.

'You were around at the time of the murder, right?'

'Of course.' She took a long drag and blew the smoke from the corner of her mouth.

'Then you must know what happened. You always know everything.' Or make it up, but it couldn't hurt to ask.

To my astonishment, Isabelle fell for my flattery, smiling as though I'd discovered a great secret. '*Bien sûr*, I've always known. But do they listen to me? Oh no. "Too neat" is what they said. How can it be too neat? If it fits, it fits, right?'

'What fits?' Léon asked, frowning.

'Suicide, of course! Everyone hated her. Maybe her lover finally came to his senses, too, so that's why she did it there.'

The frown on Léon's face only deepened. 'Why would she do that the day before the competition she so desperately wanted to win?'

Scoffing, Isabelle demolished her cigarette butt with the toe of her shoe. 'What's more important, winning a contest or losing love? I mean, I can't know everything, you know.' With that, she disappeared back inside.

I rubbed my temples. 'I've talked to three men and one woman, and they all say more or less the same. Nobody knows. They don't even seem to care much. It's too long ago.' I looked at Léon, hoping for his blessing in giving up. I didn't want to investigate now any more than when Véronique first asked me. He must see that this was a never-ending story?

But Léon was more optimistic. 'There's still this Cédric to talk to. And Margot Moulin, if she answers my email.'

I almost groaned, but the sigh I tried instead turned into a coughing fit.

'Only if you're feeling up to it, of course.'

So tempting! I could use my cold to get out of this whole thing and just spend the next few days in bed. Sounded like paradise. But then I'd lose my chance to prove to Léon that I was willing to do anything to keep him in my life. He'd go back to Véronique to comfort her in a loss she'd felt for the past thirty years. Thinking about how she'd feel, I couldn't give up yet, as much as I wanted to. I really groaned that time.

'I'll be fine,' I croaked. 'But I have my appointment first.'

I'd consider my feelings later. Right now, I had to put my business hat on.

11

Who would break in here just to rehang a painting?

The meeting with the contractor went mercifully quickly. The few last details they required I could give them without too much thinking. They'd start demolition the day after, the ugly mural being the first thing to go. Léon and I hung around the lobby after the contractor had left.

'So the restaurant is going to be the focus of this place?' Léon asked, inspecting all the nooks and crannies of the lobby, as I had done the first time I came in. The place had been closed for as long as I could remember, but Jeanette's plans were sound.

'It is. The food at the café is the only thing keeping the place in the black. A bigger venue will certainly bring in more customers because she now often has to turn people away. We're going to restore as much of the art deco bits as we can in the lobby and the restaurant in the back. The rooms upstairs will be converted so that every one of them has something unique.' I stifled a laugh, then coughed. My voice was getting that same quality Isabelle's had after years of smoking. 'One will have a jacuzzi in the middle of the room. One will be filled with plants like some kind of jungle. One will have a bed shaped like a boat, and in one' – I let out a sheepish laugh – 'Jeanette thinks it's a good idea to install a trapeze. I know she has a circus theme in mind, but...'

'Your brain made different associations,' Léon finished my thought. He grinned at me, and I hid my overheating face, wishing I hadn't said anything. Fortunately, he was on the other side of the lobby, straightening a painting of a giant vase of flowers.

I paled. 'I straightened that yesterday.'

He took his hand off the frame. 'I'm sorry. I can assure you it was crooked.'

'That's what I mean.' I stumbled towards him and the painting. 'It was also on a different hook. See that screw in the wall above? That didn't show yesterday. Someone has been in here.' But for what? Could it have been the contractors?

Léon lifted the painting off the wall to look behind but shrugged. 'Nothing there, as far as I can tell.'

Impatiently flapping my hands, I ordered him, 'Take it off.' Though he did as I said, I realised I might be a tad bossy towards Thibault, and it had become a habit. I'd have to revisit my tyrannical tendencies later, but right now, I had other things to worry about. The painting came off the wall to reveal... 'Nothing.'

'Nothing on the back of the painting either. Can you see something missing?'

I glanced around, though I hadn't noticed anything off during our rounds with the contractor. 'Not that I can see. But there's nothing of value here. Who would break in here just to rehang a painting?'

'Yet they have. You must be missing something.'

His perfectly reasonable assumption made me shiver, and I cast him an anxious look. 'I don't understand. The building has been empty for ages. If there was something interesting in here, why not get to it before?'

Probably sensing that I was about to freak out, Léon came closer. 'It's probably nothing. You've recently bought the property. Maybe they were just curious to see if anything had changed yet?'

'So they moved one painting?'

'They might have moved more, but this is the only thing you noticed. If nothing is missing or broken, though, I don't think you have to worry about it.'

That just made me worry more. Why would someone take the trouble to break in if all they wanted was a tour? We – or at least Jeanette – had been loud and proud about the new venture, so people in the village would know to ask if they wanted to see inside. Did that mean this was done by an outsider? But then curiosity made even less sense. As did any other reason I could come up with for someone to break into an abandoned hotel.

'Hey!' Léon snapped me out of my spiral of questions. 'It's all right. We'll find out what happened. Maybe Jeanette moved the painting for some reason.'

I wasn't convinced, and Léon took my hand. 'Do you want to go round again? See if anything else stands out?'

Ignoring the tingling his touch sparked, I nodded, and he guided me to the kitchen, his hand on the small of my back. At first, nothing seemed out of the ordinary.

'Oh!' I raced to the side door, where one of the little glass panes had been broken to create a hole big enough for someone's hand. The key still rested on the inside of the lock. 'I thought about taking the key from the lock, but then I thought, you know, it's been there for thirty years. Who would break in now? But then they did.'

Why?

Léon rubbed his chin. 'It does seem odd. You said you haven't changed anything yet?'

'No, we've only cleared the rubble and the spider-webs. Didn't add anything, didn't take anything away. It's a cleaner version of what's been here forever.'

Léon took my hand, and we inspected every other room in the hotel, but they were undisturbed as far as I could tell.

We returned to the lobby, staring at the old painting leaning against the wall. Léon picked it up.

'Is there anything special about this thing? It doesn't look valuable to me, but I'm no expert.'

'I think they would have taken it with them if it was. The burglar, but also the original owners when they left. We bought the hotel from the council, so if nobody thought it good enough to take in thirty years, it must not be what the burglar came for either. But then why move it?'

When Léon tried to hang the painting in its original spot, the hook turned upside down. 'At least we know why they didn't put it back there.'

'That doesn't really reassure me.'

'I know.' He hung the painting on the lower nail and turned around to lay his hand on my arm. I wished he'd hug me. In general, but especially right now. 'But I honestly don't think it's something to get upset about. Nothing's stolen or damaged aside from the glass in the door, so maybe they just broke into the wrong building by mistake?'

We both knew that was a ludicrous suggestion. Even from the back, it was obvious that this building was different from the ordinary houses surrounding it. But at that moment his phone rang.

'It's Véronique. Are you okay? Can I take this?'

I nodded reluctantly, and he went into the back. No, I was not okay. With the shock of this discovery, I hadn't noticed my headache for a while, but now I realised it was still there, quietly growing like the Blob. I moved towards the door, wondering if Léon would see me if I went outside for some fresh air, but the quibbling voices of a couple stopped me. They were just outside the door, probably seeking shelter from a sudden shower I'd seen through the w indow.

'I'm not turning my ancestral home into a tourist trap!'

'I was thinking more boutique hotel or stylish B & B. There are plenty of *gîtes* around already.'

'Exactly, so we don't need any more.'

I grinned as I recognised the haughty voice of my brother David, who occupied a giant villa all by himself. Apart, of course, from his lodger, Maëline, whom he was not at all interested in. Nuh-uh, not him. He'd only taken her on a holiday to the Caribbean 'to take her mind off things'. Who did he think he was fooling?

I pushed the revolving door and joined in their conversation. 'You're not thinking of putting me out of business before I've even started, are you?'

Maëline, who had her back to me, jumped. 'Julie! No, of course not. But the house is so big, and right now the space is wasted.'

'I thought you said it was cold and empty?' I couldn't help tease her with her own words. Because Maëline herself saw nothing in David. Not her. No way.

She shrugged. '*Eh bien*, it has its warm corners.'

'It's majestic,' David stated.

'And what purpose do *you* think would befit Her Majesty?' Maëline asked him. 'Perhaps you should just have a large family to fill it.'

The silence that followed was so heavy, I almost gasped for air.

'There's always the empty outbuildings,' David said after a few long seconds, choosing to ignore her remark. 'I don't care about them. You can do what you like there.'

The rain had stopped, and they continued their back-and-forth across the square, without even thinking to say goodbye.

I smiled at their backs, silently thanking them for taking my mind off the burglary. Now that I was outside the building, I could get a bit more perspective. I still hated the fact that someone had entered my property without permission, but the impact had been minimal. We would have to replace the locks anyway, and in fact that whole back entrance would be widened, so I didn't care about the broken glass. The only thing that still bothered me, though, was why. The fact that I couldn't come up with one good reason irked me.

I messaged my one shady contact. Maybe Thibault would know why someone would break in and not take anything. If not experience, he at least had more knowledge about these things, having been brought up in a family full of crooks. In fact, I still had a sneaking suspicion he wasn't telling me everything. I had to trust that was for the best, but trust had been an issue with me during the past few years. Only yesterday it had become apparent that I couldn't even trust myself.

The door behind me creaked, and Léon joined me. A frown on his face, he stared at the people on the square hurrying around puddles. 'That was Véronique.'

'*Oui*, you said.' I waited for more, but Léon was not done staring.

'How about lunch?' he surprised me by asking, indicating the café on the other side.

'Only if you let me pay this time.'

It was a bit early for lunch, but I got the idea that Léon wanted to discuss something. The upside was that we were served very quickly, so we already had a drink in our hands when Léon asked, 'So photography wasn't enough for you?'

'Oh, you mean the hotel? That's really more Jeanette's project. I'm almost a silent partner, although she will listen to anything I have to say. So far, I have commented on the style of dining chair, the colour of the coat rack, and whether or not we should have an aquarium in the lobby. All her business and

marketing ideas and plans are solid, so it was an easy investment to make. For me, I just hope...'

I paused. Did I want to bare my soul like that? I had done
it before, and he already knew all about me, but what I'd told
him was in the past now. I still bore the scars of my time with
Franck, but they weren't open wounds any more. What I
hoped to achieve with the hotel was almost a silly little thing
compared to what I'd already lived through, and the last
thing I wanted was for Léon to perceive me as shallow.

Léon's raised eyebrows spurred me on, but I took a different direction.

'Jeanette deserves for this to be a success. She's at the
centre of the community, along with my mother and my
brother.'

'What does your brother do?'

He'd have to wait for his answer because our food arrived. Jeanette served us herself so she could ask me how
the meeting went, skipping back to the kitchen after my
confirmation of tomorrow's schedule.

'I can see why you'd want to invest. I take it the chef is
part of the deal?' He'd had a taste of Théo's cooking the
day before and had already taken a mouthful of today's
blanquette de veau.

I nodded enthusiastically, tucking into my *quenelles*, a regional speciality of large, oval dumplings, in this case paired

with cheese and chicken. The soft texture was exactly what my throat needed.

'Everybody knows my brother will take over from my mother at some point. I mean, that won't be for years because she's far too involved with everything to give up being the mayor, but he's always at the council meetings, whereas they put me right to sleep. The village is better off with him there.'

I grinned, hoping he wouldn't see through me and find the big question there: what had I done for the village? That was my 'shallow' insecurity. Now that I was back in Saint-Maurice, the weight of the family legacy rested heavily on my shoulders. I was no good at being a public figure. But if I could get the hotel going, I would indirectly help several businesses in the village. Would that be enough? I'd already run away once. How could I ever make up for that?

I knew how that would sound to anyone else, though. If you've not been brought up to believe your family has a duty to the community, it's easy to turn your back on it. That's what I thought after *Papa* died, and what Franck encouraged. The village would be fine without me. Of course it would be! It had been. But I was a Belmain. This was my village. I had to do something. If only to prove Franck wrong.

But Léon did not need to know about all of those considerations. Instead, I made sure the subject was closed by asking, 'How is Véronique?'

The tiniest dark cloud passed over his face. If I hadn't secretly hoped to see it, I might have missed it. 'She's very excited about your involvement. She certainly believes in your capabilities.'

'That's nice.' That made one person, then. Give me a camera, and I'll show you all that can be done with it. That's where *I* believed my capabilities lay. This whole solving murders business was not my new hobby.

'She's on her way, actually.' The hesitation in his voice was palpable. 'She would like to see the hotel too.' He gently put his fork down to focus on me. 'She's convinced the break-in is related to her mother's murder. Frankly, Julie, if this is all too intense for you, I wouldn't blame you if you wanted to quit.'

Yes! This was it. My moment to gracefully retreat. 'I'll be happy to show her around the hotel first, but I think you're right. There is no new evidence, so there is no chance of a solution. I'll tell her that afterwards.'

We both smiled at each other, congratulating ourselves on saving the day. At least, that's how I felt. No more looking into a hopeless case. Just a nice meal with an old friend.

'Dessert?' I offered, but Léon's phone buzzed.

'Oh,' he said instead of '*Fondant au chocolat*, please'. 'Margot Moulin has just confirmed that she can see us this afternoon. She sounds quite excited, actually.'

'Oh,' I echoed. But then I saw the sunny side – more time with Léon. 'Well, we could just visit her. Does she give an address?'

He read it out, and I pulled it up on my map app. A new message caught my attention. My film photography friends had told me what kind of solution to use on Jeanette's old picture, but if I wanted, I could leave it with them for an afternoon, and they'd take care of it. 'If we do go there, I could drop off something for a friend on the way?'

Léon shrugged one shoulder. 'No harm in visiting a lonely old lady. I had no other plans, anyway.' The way he smiled, though, convinced me that he took it as an excuse to spend more time with me too. Whether that was true or not, I'd take i t.

'Fondant au chocolat?' was my hopeful suggestion.

The café door opened, and I groaned. No such luck.

12

Nothing much has changed around here since the Revolution

'Coucou, chéri.'

Léon diligently kissed his girlfriend, while I reined in my green-eyed monster.

'Bonjour, Véronique. Any chance you'd like a *fon—*'

'You're Véronique de Vigan, aren't you?'

Oh good, the Véronique fan club. Yves had come in behind Véronique and joined our little party before she had the chance to sit down. If she was going to at all. It looked more like she'd come to collect us.

'That's me.'

'My name is Yves. I've heard your story and just wanted to say I'm behind your decision not to give up. You have a right to know what happened to your mother.'

Eyebrows halfway across his forehead, Léon looked at me.

'My neighbour's grandson,' I explained, but how that explained anything, I wasn't sure.

Véronique, however, beamed a radiant smile at the newcomer. 'Thank you. That means a lot, coming from a local. I mean, you are...?'

'I'm Auguste Prunille's grandson,' Yves declared with obvious pride.

Other than a slight narrowing of her eyes, Véronique didn't give anything away. 'Well, Yves, *je te remercie*. It's good to know I'm not alone in this.' The biting words were obviously meant for Léon and maybe even for me, so I waved at Jeanette to bring us the bill. Time for a little action instead of just words. Perhaps, if she saw the hotel and realised it was unrelated to her mother, she'd come to her own conclusions.

I stood up. 'Why don't we go and see if the hotel holds any clues?'

Véronique now directed her rays at me. 'Thank you, Julie. I'm sure that'll be enlightening.'

'Can I come?'

I blinked at Yves's unexpected question, but saw no reason why not, so I shrugged. 'The more the merrier.'

The two of them raced across the square, Yves declaring his full support in all the ways he could think of. Léon and I followed at a distance, like parents who'd seen one too many playgrounds.

'I've always wanted to have a look inside,' Yves as he entered the building and began meticulously checking out every corner.

Véronique, however, marched straight to the back and up the stairs. Léon and I exchanged a look, then hurried after her. She stood in the dimly lit corridor, counting doors. Or at least, that's what it looked like she was doing.

'Roni?'

'Do you know which one was hers?' There was an urgency about her that reminded me of Léon's word for it – obsession.

'Whose?' Did she think her mother stayed at the hotel? Why would she, when she lived in the village?

'Margot Moulin. Who else?' Véronique's eyes told me I was an idiot for not understanding, but idiot or not, I still didn't understand.

'Why do you want to know that? And no, I've no idea in which room she stayed.' All this nonsense was getting on my nerves. I thought it was my brain being slowed by my cold, until I saw Léon's frown.

'Roni, what is it you expect to find? You'd better start being honest about this because I've had just about enough of your behaviour.'

Wow. The professor was coming through strong. For half a second, I wondered if he'd be a strict parent, but Véronique's deep sigh brought me back to the moment.

She folded her arms in front of her and cast her gaze to the threadbare carpet. 'Don't get me wrong – I still want to find out who killed my mother.' Another sigh. 'But.'

If the pause after that one-word statement was for dramatic effect, she rather overdid it.

'My mother always told me to keep my most valuable asset till last, or something to that effect. The way she said it – and because she always said it when she went to see Moulin here at the hotel – made me think she hid something valuable here.'

Léon's frown deepened, and he wrinkled his nose. 'So this whole pursuit has actually been about finding some kind of hidden treasure?'

'Well, not entirely.' She unfolded her arms to make a weighing gesture but avoided his gaze. 'Of course I want to find out what happened to Mum, but she has been gone for most of my life. If this – whatever it is – is still here, then it should be mine, right?'

'You think there is something valuable in one of these rooms. That hasn't been taken out when they closed for business?' I was so confused. The picture in my mind had too shallow a depth of field. Only a tiny part was sharp, but the rest was out of focus.

'It must be. I looked downstairs, but it wasn't there, so it must be up here somewhere,' Véronique said.

I needed sleep. 'When did you—'

'*You* broke in?' Léon interrupted me.

'Oh, I'm sorry about that.' Véronique put her hand on my arm. 'I'll pay for the damages, now I know it's yours.'

'I can't believe you dragged Julie into this... this treasure hunt!' Léon was ready to explode. 'Julie, I'm sorry *I* dragged you into this. Please accept my sincerest apology. I had no idea *this* was behind it.'

All I could do was blink while I tried to catch up. Véronique had broken into the hotel, looking for treasure she believed her mother hid when Margot Moulin stayed here? 'But the hotel stayed in business for several years after that last *concours*. Margot Moulin can't have been the last person to stay in that room.'

'I would still really like the chance to have a look. Please?'

'I suppose—'

'It'll have to be another time,' Léon cut in. 'We have an appointment with an old lady because of you. At least we won't have to upset her by talking about the murder. And don't think I have any intention of asking after your treasure.' He spat the word out like it tasted of earwax.

'Léon...' Véronique pleaded, but he strode past her and down the stairs.

I followed, feeling like I should apologise for some reason. Maybe I'd understand what had happened after I'd taken some more painkillers.

Yves came up to us in the lobby with a happy smile on his face and addressed Véronique. 'Great place this. You all done? Can I walk you home? Your father lives close to my grandfather.'

Véronique quietly accepted, and I joined Léon outside. He gave me an odd look, filled with regret.

'It's not your fault,' I tried to reassure him. 'And I don't mind, honestly.'

I was granted a half-smile for my words, but the sadness remained.

'We'll be gutting the place. If there's anything there, we'll find it.'

'You won't.' He sighed. 'I thought she wanted to know the truth about her mother's death, but it turned out to be nothing but greed. For some made-up "valuable" her mother alluded to. She doesn't even know what it is. Of course she doesn't. She was six years old at the time. She must have misunderstood, but here she is looking for it. Very disappointing.'

He looked worse than I felt, which was saying something. The poor man must love her very much to go through all of that. In his place, I'd want to be alone right now, so even though it went against my own wishes, I asked, 'Do you want to cancel our meeting with Margot Moulin?'

His eyes narrowed. 'Do you?'

Trick question! I didn't care about Madame Moulin, but I wanted to spend more time with Léon. 'Not really.'

'Let's go then.'

I picked up Jeanette's photograph to hand over to my friends in Villefranche and dived back behind the wheel. I'd knocked back some more aspirin and frankly couldn't believe my luck that I got to spend more time with Léon. Though there was plenty on my mind, my sluggish brain wouldn't let me find the right words, so I handed the envelope to Léon and started the car, reversing out of my drive.

My nose tickled. I wiggled it, but the tickle got worse. A sudden sneeze made me jerk the wheel and we jumped back towards my magnolia tree. I slammed on the brakes and managed to halt us right before we hit the tree. Eyes wide and panting, I gripped the steering wheel.

'Would... you like me to drive?'

I sneezed in answer, and we switched seats. I went round the back of the car while he rounded the front so he couldn't see my embarrassed glow. I ran an antibacterial wipe over the steering wheel and made sure to have a tissue ready the rest of the way.

Too ashamed to talk about anything meaningful, I asked Léon if much had changed since he'd left.

He chuckled. 'It's France. Nothing much has changed around here since the Revolution. That scared us so much that we've been fighting change ever since. You know why there was such a huge Resistance movement during the Second World War? Too big a change!'

He winked at me, and I laughed, pointing at the shop where I was supposed to drop off the photograph. My friends told me they'd have it ready for me within the hour, so we would be able to pick it up on the way back. The rest of the drive was quiet. Not laden, but quiet. The aspirin kicked in and cleared my mind somewhat, so I felt more human again. But with my ability to think, the questions also returned.

I started to wonder if there could be any truth to Véronique's suspicions. If Louanne *had* hidden something in the hotel, that could be a clue to why she was killed. It seemed incredible that anything that had been left behind would still be valuable today. Especially if it was cash, since it would have been left before the introduction of the euro. Then again, where could Louanne have hidden any amount of cash that wouldn't have been found in the meantime? She was not an employee at the hotel, so there were only so many places she would have had access to. The more I thought about it, the more I had to agree with Léon. This investigation wasn't going to lead anywhere.

'So what do we talk about?' I asked as Léon parked the car. The address Margot Moulin had given us was for an assisted living facility on the other side of Villefranche.

He shrugged. 'This place being what it is, we may have to congratulate her on her birthday every five minutes. Let's see how she is first.'

As it happened, 'she' was excited to see us. Margot Moulin was a stout lady in her eighties, dressed to the nines in a navy suit that threw me at first. She looked every part the capable businesswoman, but she greeted us with the words, 'So good to see you again.' When she referred to her flat as 'this hotel' and told us she only had half an hour for us before her meeting started, it became clear that she wasn't all there any more.

'Have a seat, have a seat.' She waved us to an immaculate charcoal-coloured couch and offered us coffee and a piece of *galette des rois*. Though I wouldn't ordinarily drink coffee and eat frangipane pie at two o'clock in the afternoon, I didn't want to throw her off course, so I accepted, and so did Léon.

'Now, let's see. Where do you normally start... My first business? I'm sure you already know all about that. And my current business is booming, as you know.'

With that bit of information on her state of mind, I had a brain wave. 'Actually, we were hoping to talk to you about your free time. Our article focusses on how women in power stay calm during stressful times. What do you do to unwind?'

'Oh! How delightful. Let's see… I do like to read. Thrillers, mostly. And espionage. Very exciting. But I don't get much time to do that, really. There's always someone who needs my attention on something or other.'

'You must get invited to so many events and parties as well.' Nudge, nudge.

Margot Moulin laughed. 'Oh yes! Not a week without champagne! It's a shame, though. What I really enjoy doing is going to cooking shows and contests, to judge the local cooks and bakers on their talents and skills.'

Bingo! I nodded encouragingly, and Margot took the bait.

She clasped her hands together over her chest. 'You won't believe the dishes I get to sample sometimes. There's this one woman who makes a *saucisson au gène*…' She closed her eyes and moaned, just thinking about its tastiness. 'I never can get her to share the recipe with me, but I'm sure it contains Madeira and truffle. And pistachio, of course. She always serves it with *pommes de terre vigneronnes*. The best choice, in my opinion. I mean, this is a pork sausage we're talking about. What better to pair it with than bacon? Do you know how to make a *saucisson au gène*?'

Without waiting for an answer, she launched into a monologue on the best way to combine lean pork meat with lard and pork loin to create the perfect sausage meat. Then she decided we needed to know the best ratio of potato to smoked *lardons* in how much stock and wine for making *pommes de terre vigneronnes.*

'But perhaps it's just so good because she uses her own grapes and wine for the sauce. Claudine's married to a wine grower, you see?'

'Claudine?' Léon asked. 'Don't you mean Louanne?'

Margot deflated a bit. 'Ah, yes, Louanne's is better, of course. It's such a shame that I don't have time these days to judge at contests. I think I should get back to it. Don't know why I stopped. Did you want to hear about my first restaurant? Though I'm sure you know all about it.'

We got the story anyway, and she started the cycle again before I could put a word in.

'Do you remember François Simon? He was a contestant in one of the competitions you judged, and he remembers you fondly.'

Margot's eyes narrowed as she tried to remember.

'He was a terrible cook, apparently?' I hoped that would stir things up.

An amused smile spread over Margot's face before she broke into a laugh. 'Ah, yes, poor old Monsieur Simon! Nobody around him dared tell him how bad his cooking was, but I think he knew.'

I glanced at Léon to see what he thought. François would not have been old when she met him. But Léon was enjoying his *galette* and smiling at the old lady, who shook her head with a smile.

'He came to see me afterwards. Brought a young woman he said was his wife but...' She looked confused. 'His wife had died? And he was so old... Or maybe it was that cute man at the *buvette*?'

Léon had finished his *galette* and decided to put a stop to Margot's rambling, since it didn't look like it was going anywhere any more. 'This has been enlightening, Madame Moulin. We have plenty of material to use for our article now, so thank you. I'm sure you're very busy, so we'll leave you in peace.'

Acknowledging that her diary was indeed quite full, Margot gave us a professional smile and brought us to the door. 'Thanks for visiting. I enjoyed our talk. Maybe I will think about judging contests again. I never took a bribe, you know. All right? Bye-bye now. Bye.' And with that, she closed the door behind us.

Léon and I were left staring at each other.

'Where did that come from?' I asked.

'If I were inclined to spend any thought on this matter, I'd say that was highly suspicious.' He frowned at the closed door. 'But again, whether she did or didn't take bribes, it's not going to lead us closer to finding a perpetrator.'

On our way back to the car, I asked, 'You don't think the bribe could have led to a motive?'

'Like if she were promised a bribe and didn't get it?'

'Or got it and then didn't want to be exposed?'

He thought about that. 'I suppose it's possible. I know Véronique is going to say the bribe is still at the hotel.'

'Demolition starts tomorrow. I guess we'll see.'

Neither of us particularly wanted to talk about the murder any more, so I told Léon all about the plans for the hotel. Whereas all those years ago its purpose had simply been to accommodate people who came to the Beaujolais for the wine and the landscape, Jeanette and I now hoped that the hotel itself would be enough to draw people in if we made it sufficiently attractive.

We stopped by the photography shop to pick up the picture Jeanette had given me. The shop was closed when we arrived, but there was an envelope stuck to the door, containing the photo and a note.

This was all we could do. Stain had been on there too long.

I glanced at the picture without much enthusiasm. It did look clearer now. I recognised the hotel lobby and some faces from when I was little, but a large part of the photo was still obscured by discolouration. I sent a text thanking my friend for trying, but slid the photo back in the envelope and had forgotten about it by the time Léon dropped me at my front door.

'Would you like to come in?' I asked, but my voice was so croaky from all the talking I'd done, that he declined with a smile.

'I think you should get some rest. Big day tomorrow.'

'Will I see you there?' It was a ridiculous request. Why would he be interested in seeing the inside of my old hotel being demolished?

But he didn't bat an eyelash. '*Bien sûr.* See you in the morning.'

13

Wider or tighter?

I sat in my living room, mesmerised by a cobweb flowing gently in a breeze I didn't feel. I ignored its silent call of 'clean me' and let myself be inspired by the soft rolling of the gossamer weave to do absolutely nothing.

However, since doing nothing gets boring much more quickly than you'd think, I padded to the kitchen in my fluffy socks to get myself a snack. I stuffed a few dates with cream cheese and settled in under a blanket on the couch for a nice quiet night. Of course, dairy and a sore throat don't go together, so after a coughing fit, I left the dates for what they were and opened my book again.

In strolled the blond menace. 'What are you doing?'

'I'm tidying.'

'Looks more like reading to me.'

'Okay, first, why do you ask if you already think you know the answer, and second, I have to read this so I can give it away. Where have you been, anyway?'

'Family emergency.' He shrugged and didn't elaborate.

That was the worst answer he could have given a curious person. Not that I'm a naturally curious person, mind. But with answers like that...

'Everyone okay?'

He only shrugged again, leaving me to assume nobody had died, at least. 'How's Cactus?'

'His name is Léon.' I kept my eyes on my book in the hope that Beau would get the message, but whether he did or not, he ignored it.

'I don't get it. What's so special about him?'

'You wouldn't understand. You're just a boy. He's a man.' Maybe if I were deliberately nasty, he'd get the message. After an active day when I should have been in bed, the nastiness flowed freely, but as usual, it bounced right off him.

'You've had other "men" around. Whether they're married, or gay, or with one foot in the grave, you always flirt. The only other person you don't flirt with is your brother. And me.'

'Same thing. And you flirt enough for ten.'

'Come on, *ma poule*,' he crooned. 'Tell me the big secret about Cactus.'

My chin rose, though my eyes were glued to the pages. 'I am not your chicken and I have nothing to say on the matter.' But my traitorous mouth added, 'And stop calling him Cactus. With this unsexy cold, I'm in no danger of being kissed.'

Thibault's eyes rounded, and his mouth fell open in the biggest grin. 'You're in love with him! How can you be in love with him? You've only met him yesterday. And it's... *him.*'

'Stop talking about him as if you know him.' The book finally dropped to my lap. 'I told you what he did for me.'

'Yes, but that was years ago, in a totally different situation. Do you really still know him that well?'

'I can't help how I feel!' Why was I now defending my-self? 'And who are you, Doctor Love? I'm not taking advice from the Prince of Perfunctory Pleasure.'

For some reason, that pierced his thick skin. His smile disappeared, and he cast his gaze to the floor. I immediately regretted my words. 'I'm sorry. I'm not feeling well. I didn't mean it.' Though I kind of did. Who was he to lecture me about being in love? Or about flirting with everyone. I'd only met one person besides myself who was immune to him, in her own words – Celine, the baker's daughter. That adorable girl had been friends with him since he was seven. I only met him when he was fourteen, but that was also before this overly confident personality developed. Perhaps it helped if you'd seen him as the greasy-haired, gangly teenager.

'Do you like dates with cream cheese?' I fluttered my hand at the plate. 'They make me cough.'

He took my peace offering to one of the armchairs and stretched himself diagonally across it. I finally picked up my book again.

'How can you read that dumb stuff?'

With a frustrated and slightly gargling sigh, I put my book back down. Apparently, he still had to get back at me somehow, despite the dates. 'I read romance. It's not dumb. Everybody needs a little romance in their life. Franck's wasn't real. At least this unreal "stuff" still gives me goosebumps. Besides, this is Tiana's latest. I have to read it to review it online. A friend's request with mutual benefits, is how I see it.'

His answer to that was a disinterested grunt. He popped another date in his mouth and started doodling in one of the sketchbooks he always left lying around. Even in my house. I'd already given up trying to remove them because the stream of drawing paper was endless.

I checked the clock. '19:57.'

'What happened in 1957?'

'No, the time!'

'Oh, I thought your cold case had got even colder.'

In a way, it had. Now that I knew more about the victim, I wished I *had* found something new. Louanne might not have been a popular person, but to become an anecdote, as François had called her... She deserved justice, but I didn't see how I could give her that.

Once again, I took up my book, but my heart wasn't in it any more. According to romance novels, the world was full of handsome young billionaires. Also earls, the billionaires of British yesteryear. Jane Austen had no idea what she'd unleash when she wrote the original billionaire romance – *Pride and Prejudice.*

My phone double-pinged. The first notification was a message from Tiana. *That moment none of your friends want to talk to you because they're all reading your new book.*

The answer was easy. *I think you should stop complaining and let me read.*

Notification number two was an email from Jacqueline, containing the scanned police files on Louanne's case. All right, so I wouldn't be reading Tiana's book just now. Quickly scrolling through the pages, I didn't see anything I hadn't already heard from the people I'd talked to. I'd give the files a better read in a moment, but the email had reminded me that I also needed to update Jeanette on her photo.

I'd scanned the cleaned picture this afternoon and saved it to the cloud, but I hadn't sent it to Jeanette yet. I opened it on my laptop, cropping the photo so it didn't have the stain on it. The quality improved, but the subject was still boring. I compared the two pictures, but couldn't make a decision.

'What do you think, Beau? Wider or tighter?'

'Whatever you're talking about, the answer is always tighter.'

Two clicks, and the cropped photo was on its way to Jeanette.

Now, back to the police files.

My phone pinged. I ignored it. Because I'm not a curious person, you see?

It pinged again. Probably just a corrected typo.

But what if someone was trying to reach me?

They'd call.

Ping.

Oh, for crying out loud! I grabbed my phone and almost growled WHAT at it.

Hi.

Feeling better?

Just looked up your neighbour. I think you should too.

'Why, thank you, Léon. Because of your message, I do now feel better,' I mouthed to myself so Thibault couldn't hear.

My fingers flew across the screen. Social media... Anne-Bonny... Oh. My. Yes, that vaguely resembled one of my poses. But I always told my clients to look surprised. If you lift your skirt and you don't look surprised, you get... this. Maybe it was an ad for lingerie? I checked the description. Nope, it was in fact the hardly visible skirt she was praising.

Another few fashion shots had nothing to do with me, but a video of her falling into a little stream made me laugh because it was obviously in reference to one of my poses, but this tumble didn't look staged. In fact, that tree looked awfully familiar. And that was definitely the rock in my garden! The little... *influencer* had wandered her shiny blue platform boots into *my* garden to mimic *my* photos. At least she'd tagged me in this one. About an hour ago, when the video was months old. Nobody plunges themselves in the water in January, not even an influencer looking for likes. I hoped. But she must have known who I was before she even moved here, which made her a much better actor than I would have given her credit for.

I wondered if Beau had seen through her. As I narrowed my eyes at him, Léon sent another text.

Yours are better ;)

Too right! I had things to say about it, and Léon was going to be the one to hear them. *They're too light. It's the shadows that make the portrait interesting. In books and in real life, people's dark side gives them depth of character. It's the same with photographs. Without the shadows, the picture feels flat.*

Shadows... I stared at the wall on the other side of the room, trying to excavate the hint of something that was showing in my mind. I had seen a shadow. Where it shouldn't have been. Now where was that? It was just now. What had I been doing? Anne-Bonny's pictures... The police files...

Jeanette's photo! I toggled back to the uncropped picture, staring at the stain. Then I called my mother.

'Hi, *ché*—'

'*Maman*, the ugly mural in the hotel. Was it there at the time of the murder?'

My mother uttered some unintelligible sounds, then paused. 'I... Gosh, what a question. I don't know... Err... no! No, there used to be a wall of lockers. They had that mural painted in a final attempt to draw in more customers. Why an ugly mural would—'

'*Merci, Maman!*' I'd hung up and redialed before she could finish her sentence. I'd apologise in the morning. This could be a breakthrough!

'Véronique?'

'Julie? Hang on. Dad, can you turn down the TV? Julie, I'm back.'

'You may be right. Behind the mural in the hotel is a block of lockers. Now, do understand, the chances of them not clearing the lockers before having a mural painted over them is slim, but that mural is coming down tomorrow. *If* there is something there...'

I had to stop talking because of Véronique's excited squeals on the other side of the line. 'I knew it! Dad! Didn't I say?' She whooped for another minute before I could get a word in.

'They probably cleared the lockers beforehand. There's still every chance there's nothing in them.'

'Yes, yes, I hear you. No one will blame you. I can't believe I was *right*!' The last word came out at such a high pitch, I didn't think she had actually heard me.

Thibault had sat up and leaned forward with twinkling eyes. Tomorrow's demolition would be a lot more exciting than expected.

14

This contest is not normal

'I am *not* your fiancée,' Flora whisper-shouted at Nicolas when they entered the hotel lobby.

'All right, all right. I said I'll wait.'

'That's not what—'

'Capital prize, my boy!' François stood up and gestured for them to join him and the other contestants, who were seated together in a group of comfy chairs in a corner of the lobby. They each had a drink waiting for them on the little table in the middle. 'I can't wait to win this contest and claim it. I'll be as tanned as Dina when I come back. We'll be like brother and sister.'

'You'd have to learn to cook like Dina first,' Lucille scoffed. The sprightly sixty-eight-year-old always had a naughty twinkle in her eye. She didn't care what others thought of her, a trait Flora was very jealous of.

'I can teach you to make *makroudh*. Just the thing for your sweet tooth.' Dina's heavily made-up eyes fluttered their long lashes at her 'brother'. 'Have you ever been to Algeria?'

François shook his head as if she'd asked him whether he'd ever been to the poo museum. Fortunately, Dina didn't seem to take offence at his aversion.

'I have,' Nicolas declared. His job allowed him to travel with huge discounts, something he took advantage of all the time. He always asked Flora along, but she'd only gone with him on three occasions over the last two and a half years. Algeria had not been among those destinations.

Dina clapped her hands together. 'Did you like it? Did you have *makroudh*?'

Nicolas inclined his head. 'Of course. Loved the Roman ruins at Timgad.'

'Pff, tourist attraction!' Dina waved the thought away with her hand. 'We'll go together. I'll show you the real Algeria.'

Nico's smile couldn't have been wider. He was big on authenticity. Flora felt her stomach tickle as she watched him ask Dina a hundred questions about the 'real Algeria'. Would she be coming along? He seemed to think so, casting her enthusiastic glances now and then. He was so cute! But how could he assume her answer before she'd given it? Why was he so much more convinced than she?

'The prize destination is Réunion, not Algeria,' she reminded him, her voice perhaps a bit more stern and prickly than she intended.

'Anyone been to Réunion?' Nicolas asked the group as Cédric approached the table with a glass of sparkling water and an orange juice. Flora and Nico had come in often enough for Cédric to know their usual. Flora shot her friend a grateful smile. Any distraction from this conversation would do, but Cédric was a good one. She wished she could go with him and leave Nicolas to deal with the interview.

No one had been to Réunion. 'Anyone want to go to Réunion?' Nico then tried. That got a much more excited reaction. Flora made notes on a napkin for Louanne to write up later. Claudine, sipping her red wine, would use the holiday to do nothing but sit in the sun and enjoy parasol drinks. Dina would teach her children about the different climate, the geology, and animals' habitats. Lucille thought she'd like to try the local food, and François pictured himself snorkelling and swimming with turtles. With everyone describing their dream holiday, Flora found herself fantasising over what she would do on a tropical island vacation. All the activities the others described sounded amazing, but she would probably go on early morning hikes to explore the island and its marvellous volcano.

While Flora's mind was still wandering emerald mountains and turquoise seas, Nicolas had asked a question about the contest.

'Louanne,' everyone agreed was the answer to whatever he'd asked.

'*Normalement*, I would have said Claudine was my biggest worry,' Dina said, while Claudine cast her eyes down with a blushing smile. 'But this contest is not normal. Don't write that down!'

Her words reminded Flora that she was supposed to take notes, and she shook herself out of her tropical daydream. The dream would probably be better than the real thing anyway, since it didn't entail airports and sunscreen and lugging suitcases...

Lucille frowned, clutching her glass of milk as if she wanted to wring its neck. 'You're right at that. The *concours* used to have twenty contestants, easily. Now look at us. I don't even care about winning – I just want to defy Louanne. If she wins again this time, I'm staging a coup next year.'

'I care about winning,' Claudine declared with a passion. Her wine sloshed about in her glass with the force of her gesticulation. 'Did you see her this afternoon? She doesn't care. She slaps the stuff together and goes off to talk to the media. There's no way hers is better than mine.'

A few drops of wine escaped the glass and landed on her sleeve, but Claudine was seething and didn't notice.

Flora narrowed her eyes. 'But if the judges change every year, how can she still win if her *saucisson* isn't up to scratch? And what could she hope to gain if she does cheat?'

Claudine opened her mouth, but what they heard was not her answer.

'If you could be slightly less useless?' The jarringly loud voice cut through their conversation. Everyone turned to look at Louanne, who had come in with a man Flora recognised as the one Apolline and her friend had been talking to before Flora took them to Villefranche. Louanne lowered her voice when she realised she'd drawn attention, but though they could no longer hear her words, her tone towards the man had not changed. They disappeared to the back and François raised his eyebrows in a gesture of we've-seen-it-all-before.

'Makes you wonder if she was like that before they got married, or if he likes to be treated that way.'

'That's her husband?' Flora exclaimed incredulously.

'Have you never seen him in the *caveau*?' Claudine asked. 'He's always there, behind the counter.'

Flora shook her head. 'I've only been there once or twice.'

'Really?' Nicolas looked stunned.

'We usually go to Villefranche,' Flora replied, slightly piqued that he wouldn't know this about her but still be convinced he knew her well enough to know she'd marry him.

'Well, we'll have to remedy that, won't we? Tonight, we'll go to the *caveau* instead.'

Louanne's interruption had cooled the contestants' interest in talking about the competition, so after a few generic questions on their favourite foods to cook and how long they'd been interested in cooking, they rose to take their belongings out of the lockers along the back wall.

Flora remained glued to her chair, glaring at Nicolas.

Her outright annoyance seemed to finally have rocked his confidence. 'What?' he asked, more confused than concerned.

Waiting for the stragglers to leave the lobby, she crossed her arms and tapped her foot on the floor. But by the time they were alone, her anger had already given way to insecurity once more. Trying to sound more together than she felt, she explained, 'You proposed, and I didn't accept. You can't just assume everything will continue as it's done before.'

'Why not?' he asked. 'You just need a bit more time, right? I told you that doesn't bother me.'

'That's not how this works!' She got up, frustrated with her inability to explain. 'If *I* don't know if I want to marry you, *you* can't be sure about it!'

He looked truly confused then, and she couldn't take any more. Grabbing her purse, she stormed out of the hotel. This called for drastic measures – a cup of tea and the new Disney VHS she'd bought the day before. On her way to her flat, however, Louanne called out to her. Could she pretend not to have heard the shrew? She took another two steps and entered the post office. Concealed by a cardboard cut-out of a happy postman, Flora peered out through the shop window. Louanne had been flagged by Isabelle, the village gossip. Flora was safe.

'*Bonjour*, Flora. How are you today?' The sing-song voice of Claire Braymand, who ran the post office to punctual perfection, was a welcome sound. 'What can I do for you?'

'Nothing, really. I'm just hiding from Louanne, but she's caught Isabelle instead, so hopefully I'm safe for the moment. Anything new?'

La Mademoiselle, as she was known in the village, tapped the counter with her forefinger while peering through the window. 'Yes, they've been having a lot of animated discussions lately...' She changed her tone from pensive to carefree as she straightened an already straight display with today's papers. 'No, nothing new as far as I know. Unless you have something to tell me?' She stretched the word 'you' out to prompt Flora.

Could she know? How could she know? No, she couldn't possibly know. Fortunately, Flora was saved from suspicious behaviour by the shop door opening. Unfortunately, the person entering the post office was Louanne.

'Afternoon, Claire. Ah, Flora. I have a favour to ask. Could you deliver some crates of wine for me? It would have to be today, I'm afraid. It's only to Glaicé. Wouldn't take you more than half an hour.'

'Louanne, I'm—' Not in the mood? Would that count?

'Splendid. I'll see you in an hour? Don't forget!' And she sailed out the door.

La Mademoiselle regarded her pityingly. 'You're allowed to refuse, you know.'

'When, exactly, was I supposed to do that?' Flora sighed, her shoulders sagging. Sometimes it seemed she lived half her life doing things others expected of her. And that would only get worse if she married Nicolas. But if she didn't *not* want to marry Nicolas, she had better get used to it.

One hour. Not enough to watch a Disney movie. But enough for a cup of tea. With lemon, to make it taste as sour as she felt. It would have to do. She said goodbye to Claire Braymand and left the post office, where Isabelle was waiting for her. Flora suppressed a groan. Could she not get one minute's peace today?

'Did you hear?' Isabelle had a way of being opaque about things, but this was vague even for her.

'Hear what?'

'Never mind. The newcomer is waiting for you.' She pointed her thumb across the street, where François was leaning up against a little green hatchback. 'Tell him to get you himself next time,' she called over her shoulder as she left.

Flora frowned. What a baffling encounter. Was it her, or was there something wrong with everyone else today? She was bouncing from one strange request to the next with no idea where she'd end up.

Tentatively, she approached François.

'Get in the car.'

'What?'

'So no one can hear. Get in the car.'

Had she inadvertently walked through the looking-glass today? What was going on? Flora opened the door and sat in the passenger seat, while François rounded the car and got in as well.

'Is she paying you?'

What kind of a question was that? 'Who?'

'Louanne, of course. Is she paying you to deliver the bottles? Because you should know what you're in for.'

In for... Flora shook her head. She needed to wake up from this ridiculous dream. She had her hand on the door handle already and was about to leave when François put his hand on her arm.

'If you're delivering for her, just know that it won't be wine.'

With an exasperated sigh, Flora fell back in the seat. 'All right, if you're set on telling me something, I'll listen. What is with everyone today?'

'I was supposed to make that delivery for her. Bit of extra cash, you know. But Cédric found out there's something different in those bottles than what it says on the label.'

'Something like...' She raised her eyebrows at François to get him to fill her in, but he only stared at her. She'd expected him to say the wine was watered down, but this was a seriously serious stare. *Eau de vie?* He stared some more, dipping his chin low. 'What, you mean...? Drugs?' She whisper-shouted the last word at him, feeling like this was the perfect peak of weirdness for a seriously weird day. 'You're joking! Why would Louanne be handling drugs? And why would you transport them for her if you know what's going on? I don't believe you.'

Again, she reached for the door handle, but again, François stopped her. 'Cédric only recently found out. We're not even sure what's going on, but she's always paid us cash in hand from one of those big rolls you see in films. Then suddenly, she tells us she won't need us any more and she hasn't paid us for the last delivery. But now she's asked you to make one instead. For free.'

'That's not fair.' To say the least. But Flora's head was swimming with the outrageous accusations she'd just heard.

'I'm glad you see it my way. Here's what I propose. You pick up those crates, just like you said. But instead of taking them to Glaicé, you bring them to me, *tu vois*?'

Flora looked him in the eye. 'And what will you do with them?'

'You don't have to worry about that. I'll make sure—'

'No!' A strange sensation coursed through Flora's body. She didn't know why exactly she did what she did, but Francois's story was more than a little off. It was downright wrong. Something had to be done, but it wasn't simply bringing the bottles to François. She reached for the door handle one final time and opened the door. 'No, you can't do that. *I* can't do that. I won't. We'll have to stop her some other way.'

François held up his palms in desperation. 'But... how?'

Flora already had one foot on the pavement. She'd had as much as she could take today. François would have to find his own way of dealing with Louanne. She was done with everyone, and she'd make sure to use words sharp enough to get her point across. 'If you don't want to confront her, I guess you'll just have to kill her.'

She got out, only to look up into the shocked face of Nicolas. He frowned and recoiled, then turned and strode off.

15

STOP!

After a restless night of being either too hot or too cold, breathless from coughing or from a blocked nose, and generally feeling miserable, I woke to the sound of my own sneeze. The sneeze was followed by a bunch more, interspersed by ever more coughs. Wheezing, I finally sat up and brushed the gunk from my eyes.

What time was it? Dark o'clock. But according to my watch, late enough to have to get up. I stumbled to the medicine cabinet. Painkillers first, as well as nose spray and a lozenge. I groaned when I realised today would not be a contacts day. All the pictures the press would take at the start of our building works would show me in my cat-eye glasses. Good thing I wasn't vain.

I drooped into the kitchen, hoping coffee would work its magic. I needed it today. Véronique had been much too excited last night at the prospect of finding something in the lockers. I should have thought my actions through, but if I were honest with myself, the possibility of finding a new clue had clouded my reason too. It would have been better if I'd kept the information to myself and only alerted her if we actually found something.

With my mug of wake-up juice, I shuffled to the big window in my living room overlooking my garden and the vineyards beyond. The lazy sun's glow over the morning mist bathed the valley in vanilla. I slurped to greet it.

'What's with you? Morale in your socks today?'

I slurped extra loudly. 'You coming to the hotel?'

'Where else would I be?' Thibault's voice sounded muffled, which meant he was probably in the kitchen, finishing off my coffee. For one brief moment, I wondered why I still considered it *my* coffee, but then I remembered it was. Just because he drank it every morning, didn't mean he had the right to. One day, I'd kick him out.

He slurped to announce he was now standing next to me. As if I wouldn't smell that aftershave. 'Who else will catch you if you swoon?'

For once, it wasn't a rhetorical question. He wanted me to answer, but I wasn't going to say it. He was only fishing for the words so he could make fun of me. Which, of course, he did anyway.

'You know he's taken, right?'

Did he have to remind me? No. No, he didn't. He was enjoying this at my expense. One day was getting closer by the minute.

Saving himself for now, he changed the subject. 'So they'll start at nine?'

'Yes, *Maman* insisted on a big to-do. She said a big local project should have a big kick-off. So I expect the council will be there and maybe one or two members of the press, but honestly, it's not that big a deal.'

'But Léon will be there.' He put his hand over his heart and fluttered his eyelashes, so I shoved him.

'So will Véronique. She'll probably be the focus of the morning now. I doubt Jeanette is going to like that.'

He pointed his finger at me, the soft sunlight accentuating his boyishness. 'Don't you start adding suspects into the mix of my future murder investigation. If Véronique drops dead, I know it'll have been you.'

I winced. 'Don't say that! One murder in her family is bad enough. You're getting far too flippant about murder.'

'Getting?' He drained his mug and sauntered back to the kitchen.

I had to admit he was right – he'd been flippant from the start about the recent deaths. I felt a motherly comment coming on but held my tongue. Better save my energy for the rest of the day.

More and more people gathered outside the hotel. What I thought wouldn't interest anybody had brought out half the village. I stared at the crowd from inside the lobby while Jeanette chatted with the contractor. Five more minutes. Where was Léon?

Véronique had been here since before I arrived. Smiling and waving at the crowd, she'd already told them what she hoped to find. The way this was going, we might have a lot more disappointed spirits today. We'd had the contractor confirm that if the lockers were still in place, they would most likely have been emptied before the mural was put up, but Véronique didn't seem put off at all. She'd dragged Yves into the lobby and was happily chattering away. Parts of the conversation drifted my way.

'Wait, so you grow grapes, but you don't like fruit? I make a mean lemonade, you know.'

'Save it for someone else. I prefer a gazpacho.'

Neither of them seemed to miss Léon, but I checked my watch again. Though I'd left all the talking to Jeanette and didn't have anything official to do, I'd still feel better with him by my side. Or even by Véronique's side, but here, at least. I hated to admit it, but I missed the close presence of Thibault.

He, however, was near the reception desk on the other side of the room with my mother and brother, talking to her village hero, Apolline Bailly, a long-faced woman with a stern chignon and a perpetually haughty air. If I could avoid her today, that would be excellent, thank you very much. Beau knew this, and the fact that he was talking to her now was specifically to keep her away from me. Maybe I'd let him stay just a little while longer.

A man from *Le Courant* was busily taking pictures of 'the before'. He'd given me regards from his colleague, Romy Martin, who'd said she wasn't sorry she couldn't attend because she was working on a big case. I'd grinned at those words. Apparently, she'd finally been promoted from local affairs to the bigger, investigative cases. I only hoped she wouldn't regret not coming if we did find a clue today.

Two more minutes. A burly man with a giant sledgehammer had positioned himself next to the mural. He would kick off the demolition in what I considered to be an overly theatrical manner. But secretly, I wanted to be the one wielding that hammer to destroy the colourful atrocity disgracing 'my' walls. Technically, they were my walls, but they felt more like Jeanette's walls. Still, the mural had felt like a personal attack on me from the beginning, blatantly displaying itself as pictorial art where I knew my own would never hang.

One more minute. The door revolved and Léon came in. I discreetly did a little hoisting to make sure I looked perky.

'Sorry, there was a traffic jam near Ouilly.'

That was halfway between here and Villefranche. 'I thought you were staying with—'

'STOP!' A woman with brown, freckled skin and dark red hair came running into the lobby.

'Who...?' Léon started, but I held up my palms, eyebrows raised.

The woman went straight for the man with the sledge-hammer, who'd lifted it in order to deliver the fateful blow. She jerked it from his hand and hurled it across the floor, barely missing a couple of council members. 'Whew!' she said, breathing a relieved sigh before smiling at the aston-ished faces around her.

'Let. Me. Through!' Another woman stumbled into the lobby, this one harassed-looking in a charcoal-coloured business suit. Next to the first woman, who wore a flow-ing, flowery dress, she looked positively sour, although in reality that was probably due more to the fact that she'd had to struggle to get in than that it was her true nature because her face changed as soon as she saw the mural. 'Ah, yes. Exquisite.'

She couldn't mean our painting? Everyone else in the room had gazed on the spectacle with open mouths, but consciousness was starting to return, and the contractor asked Jeanette in a brusque tone I felt she didn't deserve, 'Can we get on with it?'

'No!' the business lady said. 'I'm here to prevent the loss of one of France's greatest treasures.'

I exchanged a panicked look with Jeanette. Was the building listed? Had we forgotten one of the five thousand permits we'd needed?

'This' – she indicated the ugly mural – 'is an original Luc Leduc.'

The crowd in the lobby gasped. Even I knew his paintings went for exorbitant amounts at auctions.

Apparently, though, Véronique didn't. 'Is that worth any-thing?'

Business Lady frowned at her. 'It's priceless. But it would probably fetch three to five million at auction.'

Another collective gasp. Véronique jumped up and down with glee, but then her face fell.

'What—' I whispered to Léon, but he'd already started ex-plaining.

'She's just realised it's not hers.'

I glanced sideways just in time to catch the disgusted look on his face before he schooled it.

Excited murmurs now buzzed across the room. Business Lady approached the mural and started examining it. The burly man, hands deep in his pockets, sauntered across the room, picked up his sledgehammer, and left.

Véronique stared at the mural as if it had destroyed her life, but then I caught Jeanette's incredulous eyes staring at me. She came over but needed a second to find her voice.

'I can't believe how lucky you are. Your ugly mural is worth millions.'

My mural? Ah, yes, I supposed she was right, technically. 'Oh no. I hate it. Don't you remember? I gave it to you the first time we came in here.'

I knew she'd been too excited to remember anything that happened on our first visit, apart from the plans she'd made in the moment.

'You did?' Her eyes widened, then bulged as her breath caught. 'You really did? Oh… Oh! Théo!' She ran back to her other business partner and chef, and I uncrossed my fingers.

'Don't you want three million?' Léon couldn't hide the amusement in his voice.

'Don't you think that was worth three million?' Maybe not to everyone, but it was to me. Besides, I saw it as an investment. In the hotel *and* in our friendship.

'But… what about the lockers?' Véronique spoke loudly to be heard above the hum in the room.

The time had come for action. I addressed the council members and told them there would be no demolition today. We'd have to figure out what to do first. While my mother stayed on for advice, my brother herded everyone, including Léon, out the door and informed the waiting crowd outside. I heard some disappointed noises and some cheers, but since there would be none of the promised celebratory drinks, most people just hurried home.

I turned to Jeanette, who was in conversation with the contractor and Business Lady, but then I caught sight of the woman in the flowery dress.

'So...' I began, hoping she'd offer an explanation.

'Why did I give you three million euros?' she asked with a nervous laugh.

I grinned, recognising deflection when I saw it. 'It won't be that after we subtract the cost of delay and the careful removal of the painting itself, but all right. How and why did you storm in last minute to save a painting everyone had forgotten over the last thirty years? Who are you?'

'I don't... know.' She shook her dark auburn curls. 'Well, I know who I am. My name is Jessica Rose. I'm an artist myself. I live near the abandoned petrol station. But I don't exactly know why I'm here. Someone called me yesterday evening to warn me that there was a Luc Leduc in the hotel and that it would be destroyed in the morning. I spent all night trying to figure out if it could be true and contacting anyone who'd have the authority to stop you.'

'Man or woman?'

Jessica cast an uncertain glance at Business Lady. 'Woman...?'

'No, the person who called you. Was it a man or a woman?'

'Oh!' She laughed, showing beautiful white teeth. The photographer in me couldn't help but want to reach for my camera. 'That was a man. But to be honest, I couldn't tell you much more about him. I was too stunned by his message. When I tried to call him back, he'd blocked me or something. I couldn't get through. So then I thought I might as well do some research. Turns out he was right.'

'Julie...' Jeanette waved me over, so I thanked the beautiful Jessica Rose and told her I'd be in touch.

'Since my painting is attached to your hotel, we have to make some decisions together.'

Revelling in my friend's excitement, I spent an hour saying yes to almost everything the other three proposed. The mural would be lifted by a team of specialists, cleaned, and put up for auction. As soon as it was safely removed, the demolition would go ahead as planned, but I did barter for no fanfare. I reckoned there would be enough curious faces there without our invitation. Giving in, Jeanette immediately started planning a grand opening, and I smiled, the last of my energy draining away. I needed more coffee and more painkillers. Sleep would have been better, but I could see Véronique outside, waiting for me.

16

Will it change much?

'When do you think we can get to the lockers?'

I'd tried to get past her, but since we were on the village square, there was nowhere to hide.

'Can I buy you a coffee, Véronique? I really need one.'

Léon hurried over from where he'd been talking to my brother. 'Véronique, I think you should allow Julie some time to gather her thoughts.'

She stuck her chin out at him. 'You get no say in this.'

Raising my eyebrows, I halted my dash towards the café. I expected Léon to have some sort of reply, but it seemed he was going to follow Véronique's order.

I sighed. 'I don't know yet, Véronique. We can't get to the lockers until the mural is lifted, and frankly, we all believe them to be empty. I wish I could do more for you, but I haven't found one new clue. I think it's time you accept that there's nothing I can do.'

'So I have to wait for the blasted mural to come off.'

I suppressed an incredulous growl. 'Yes, I suppose you do.'

She stalked off without a goodbye, leaving Léon to apologise for her.

I waved his words away. 'I'm sorry, but it doesn't mean much, coming from you.' I put my fingers to my temples and squeezed my eyes shut. 'I mean... *Atchoo!*'

'Exactly,' Léon agreed, handing me a tissue. 'Let's go grab a coffee.'

When he placed the cup on the table in front of me along with a glass of water, I'd already fished some aspirin from my purse.

Léon left me to stir and drink my coffee in peace before he spoke. 'That was an interesting turn of events.'

I huffed a raspy laugh. 'Unexpected, that's for sure.'

'Will it change much?'

I shrugged one shoulder. 'Not for me. Jeanette could have taken the money and waved the whole hotel project farewell, but I knew she wouldn't. It's been her dream since before we became friends. This has just made it easier.' I smiled. 'A lot easier.'

He sipped his coffee. 'It'll just take a little longer to get started.'

'It will, but the work has been postponed so many times before that this is only the latest, but certainly not the gravest, setback.'

'Oh?'

I narrowed my eyes at him. This kind of small talk was not his usual, and I was beginning to suspect he was working up to something. 'When we first bought the hotel, people were nothing but excited about our plans. But right before the work was supposed to start, some anonymous person made a complaint. They wouldn't tell us who it was or what the complaint was about, but it kept us in correspondence for months. And then suddenly, they gave up. We still don't know why. Jeanette and I have had tipsy evenings filled with conspiracy theories, but eventually, we were just happy to finally make set plans and go ahead. And now this.'

'When...' Playing with a coaster, Léon kept his eyes on the table. 'When did they stop?'

'End of October.' If only my brain would work properly, maybe I could figure out what he meant by this silence. The aspirin was starting to do its job, but there was still too much fog in my brain to see through. I'd have to let it go for now. There was something else I wanted his opinion on, though. 'I lied to Véronique.'

That got his attention. He finally looked me in the eye. 'Oh?'

'Well... sort of. I said I hadn't uncovered one new clue, but she herself in fact gave it to me.'

Léon frowned, not there yet.

'If Véronique is right, and Louanne hid something valuable in one of the hotel lockers, the motive for her murder could be greed, not jealousy or hatred as everyone assumes. I think we should have another look at the people involved in this new light.'

He leaned back in his chair. 'You still want to continue investigating?'

I bit my lip. 'I think I owe it to Louanne to explore every possibility, don't you?'

He slowly shook his head. 'I don't see how the motive could make any difference. There was never any physical evidence to connect any of them to the crime, so what changes if the motive changes?'

'It could add new suspects into the mix. People we haven't considered before because they didn't seem to have anything to do with Louanne. But if there was someone who had money trouble at the time but was solvent or even affluent after-wards...'

'Have you heard of such a person?'

He had me there. My turn to cast down my gaze. 'No.'

'Then where are you going to conjure this new suspect from?' He bent towards me, laying his hand over mine on the café table. 'Look, Julie, I'm all for finding justice. I'll gladly help you in any way I can, but do you think maybe you will have to accept there's nothing you can do?'

Somewhere in the cloud in my brain, my little voice rebelled. Had I not found an actual clue? Was there really nobody else

I could talk to? But it was drowned out by a coughing fit that made my eyes water.

'At least for now.' Léon laid his hand on my back as he pulled me up with the other. 'Please go home and take it easy for a while. Here, let me take you.'

He paid for the coffee and led me to his car. In less than two minutes, I said goodbye to him, having already promised him I wouldn't do any more sleuthing until I'd rested and felt better. It was an easy promise to make. As soon as I lay down on the couch and pulled the soft cover over my legs, I was gone.

I woke to the smell of something sweet and meaty, making my stomach growl. Sneaking into the kitchen, I spent a half-awake second watching my unwanted assistant making himself indispensable again. I wondered if Léon was any good in the kitchen. But then, who was I kidding? He already had someone else. And despite what Beau wanted me to think, I could take care of myself. I didn't need any man. But sometimes it was kind of nice to have one around.

As I opened the cupboard and reached for the plates, Thibault rapped the pan with a wooden spoon, making me jump.

'Good morning!'

What made him so cheerful? I tore off a piece of the fresh baguette and took a chair.

'Feel better?'

Come to think of it, I did. My nose wasn't clogged and my brain seemed clear. '*Oui*, I think,' I rasped, but after I'd cleared my throat, even that felt much better. I silently thanked the couch for an hour well spent.

'So, who are we interrogating this afternoon?' He filled our plates with pork stewed in dried fruit and poured himself a glass of wine. I got tea, which made me both glad and sad. But if I had tea today, I'd be back to wine tomorrow.

'Léon thinks there's nothing to investigate.'

Beau studied my face as he sat down to eat. 'But?'

'Do you think if the motive was greed, there could be other suspects?'

'Almost certainly.' He swallowed. 'Question is, who?'

'Hm.'

We ate in silence for a while, enjoying the sweet tenderloin and thinking about suspects.

'There is one person we haven't talked to yet. François mentioned Cédric,' I said.

Beau thought for a moment. Now that he'd been living with me a few months, he'd met most of the people I knew here. 'The one with the...' He motioned over his mouth and I nodded.

Cédric was known locally as Le Barbu, a title he boasted of. The natural colouring in his moustache made one side dark, the other white. Now that he was getting on in years, the dark side was getting a bit lighter, which he compensated for by growing the beard longer. He and my mother had been friends forever.

'All right, I'll come with you.'

'No more family emergencies?'

He avoided having to answer by taking another bite of his food. So, I was not to know. Which was fine. I wasn't curious. Instead of making up all sorts of theories like a curious person, I would ask him again later. For now, I was going to enjoy the little kiwi cheesecakes we had for dessert.

'I think it's that Margot Moulin. If you're now investigating greedy people, she's first in line. Why else would she tell you out of the blue that she never took a bribe?'

I wrinkled my nose. 'She doesn't know what she's saying. This came after she told us she had an important board meeting. She's lost the plot.'

'Doesn't mean she didn't do it.'

'No, but how are we ever going to prove it?'

'The perfect crime,' Beau said with a sly smile.

I thought of her years in institutions. 'Hardly. I think that goes for pretty much everyone but her. They got away with it, but she's the only one who paid a price.'

'Who else could it be?'

I raised one eyebrow. 'Isn't that what we're supposed to find out?'

'Cactus wants you to stop looking.'

'Don't call him Cactus.' And maybe Léon was right. On the surface, there was no chance I'd uncover thirty-year-old evidence. But I kept thinking that if I dug in the right place, something would turn up – because whoever had done it had got careless or comfortable along the way, or because someone who needed to be protected had passed away. Anything that would provide a new insight, or a slightly different angle on things.

'Maybe he did it, and that's why he wants you to stop looking.'

'He could barely walk at the time! If this is the kind of theory you're going to come up with, maybe you should stay out of the investigation.' We'd started the dishes and I jabbed a dripping plate at his chest.

'*Et quoi encore.* You know you need me, *ma poulette*. Yesterday, you had the perfect opportunity to put the screws on Margot Moulin, but did you come up with anything? I would have made sure to get that confession.'

'You're only making a case against yourself.' I put the cutlery in the drawer and went to put my coat on. 'What screws are you planning to put on Cédric?'

'That depends on what he does or does not confess to, obviously,' he half-mumbled as he tied a scarf around his neck. 'We're only talking to him now because we've already talked to everyone who was obviously involved. What do you expect to find out?'

He had me there. I locked the door behind us while I thought of things to ask Cédric. 'Maybe, *because* he wasn't involved, he'll have a different view of things. I think I'll just let him talk and see what happens.'

'Well, then I'll show you what screws I'll put on him when the time comes.'

I rolled my eyes as we entered the village square. A group of older teenagers saw us, and one of the boys approached Thibault.

'You're Thibault Fouquet, right?'

Beau stared him down, but the boy was clueless.

'So, err, got any tips?'

How did the boy not feel the cold radiating off of my friend? He raised his eyebrows in disdain, but his tone was casual. 'Tips?'

'You know...' The boy raised his hands and waved them up and down in the shape of a violin.

Suddenly, Beau chuckled and with an understanding 'Ahh' he took his sketchbook from his pocket and tore out a page. He wrote an address on the paper and gave it to the boy, who whooped and rejoined his friends.

My mouth fell open. 'What?!'

Thibault shrugged, enjoying my abhorrence.

'What did you write?' My pitch had veered into opera singer territory, and he truly laughed that time.

I was about to swat him when he held up his hands. 'Relax. As soon as they start the hand wiggle, I give them the address of a guitar shop in Villefranche. Happens all the time.'

Really? The hand wiggle hadn't died out in the sixties?

'Some day I'll have to go in and apologise for all the guys coming in asking for girls.'

'You'd hope they would realise they've been had as soon as they see the window display.'

He blew air from between closed lips. 'That kind? Pff! Nuh-uh. I've seen them' – he hitched his thumb over his shoulder – 'around. Always in the same formation. Checking out girls in clubs but never brave enough to talk to them. As if they bite! Well, you know.'

He grinned, and I shook my head. Sometimes, the nine years between us might as well be ninety. 'We're here, *mon lapin*.' I couldn't help using his own habits against him, but he only grinned wider.

We were let in by a little girl and found Cédric on all fours, playing horse for two of his granddaughters, of which there were many. His three daughters had borne daughters of their own, and all of them used him as a day-care centre. That's why the simple living room furniture had guards on all corners, and pink soft toys sat lined up on the couch. The man as I knew him could be a little rough around the edges but to the girls, he was a teddy bear.

'Oh, it's you' was his greeting. He made no attempt to get up or offer us a seat. 'I wondered if I'd be graced with a visit. Flora said you were investigating.'

Count on him to tell it like it is. He'd always called my mother by her name in front of me because that's who she was to him. And I always felt that in his eyes, I was still the little brat who'd caused his friend pain by running off with a criminal. But I could probably count on him not to bother with niceties about everyone else involved. He was not a gossip, but he didn't sugar-coat anything either.

So he would probably appreciate a straight-to-the-point approach. 'Anything you want to say about it?'

He rumbled a laugh that made his beard shake, but then finally took the girls off his back and got up.

'As you probably expected, I have plenty to say about it. Have a seat. Your mother hated that contest. As much as she ever hates anything.'

What he meant was that my mother always tried to see both sides of things. Except when David and I fought as children. Then we were both punished.

'Every year, for weeks on end, the whole village could talk about nothing but sausage and wine sauce. That *écervelée* of a judge came round several times beforehand to talk things over with *la reine*. Every contestant accused the next of stealing their recipe, and that last time, in strode François with all his airs. I was quite happy to see the end of that competition. Though it did make me a good extra sum.'

'I thought the whole thing was run with volunteers?' Beau asked. One of the little princesses had claimed his lap and was now playing with the buttons on his shirt. Beau didn't seem to think anything of it.

'Yes, but I ran the *buvette*. People tip extra if you spike their drinks. At their request, of course. Who'd want to be sober for such a farce?' He bellowed a laugh, but then his dark eyes turned serious. 'Somehow, Louanne found out, though. Gave me a right bol... hum... reprimand. If I didn't like her before, I really couldn't stand her after that. Someone else must have felt the same.'

'Any idea who?'

'Well, everyone felt the same. But someone must have acted on it. If I knew who, though, I would have said so at the time.'

His words didn't hold the same indignation as when François had spoken them. For Cédric, they were simply a fact.

'I don't know if you heard, but Véronique thinks some kind of valuable item or a substantial sum of money was involved. She couldn't tell us how, but we're now looking into people who could have a monetary motive.'

Cédric's eyes crinkled at the corners. 'Is that why you came to me? Because I was the poorest sod there?'

I shook my head, trying to come up with a reason for our presence that didn't sound insulting, but he took pity on me.

'I'm sure your mother knew, though she never said anything, but I had the biggest crush on her. It's a pity your dad was such a great guy because I would have loved to hate him. How could I compete with the village's biggest toff? I was only a student, and he had a cushy travel job. I still tried, though. Worked everywhere I could get my hands on some money, just to take her to some fancy restaurant. Always had at least two jobs on the go. Unfortunately for you, I never knew Louanne had left some treasure lying around. Would have been extremely tempted to take it if I had.'

'Do you know if anyone else suddenly had the money to go to that fancy restaurant?' Beau asked. The girl now stood on his legs, making little ponytails in his hair. His precious hair that I was never allowed to touch! I had to tear my gaze away to focus on Cédric's answer.

Cédric heaved a sigh. 'I can tell you're not going to take my word for it if I tell you I don't know anything, so here's my list of who was there and what I thought of them. All right?'

'That would be perfect!'

'Thought so.' He murmured something about me and my mother into his beard, but then counted on his fingers. 'One. Louanne. Awful woman. Not one person who didn't secretly or even openly sigh with relief after she was gone. She could get a saint to swear.

'Two. Gilles. Never dumped his daughter with his in-laws again after Louanne's death. With her no longer behind the counter, business in the *caveau* actually picked up.

'Three. Claudine Prunille. The person who should have won the contest, had it been fair. She was a fierce competitor. Told everyone she thought Louanne was a cheat, but she had no proof, so Louanne told her she'd sue her for slander if she didn't stop spreading lies. She would have, too, so Claudine had no choice but to back down. But Louanne knew everyone already believed her rival. She said so herself on that last night. Yes, yes, I was there. I'll get to that in a minute.'

He held up his hand in a tempering gesture that didn't do much for my patience.

'Four. Auguste. Strong rumours about an affair with Louanne, but none that I have ever seen confirmed. Frankly,

I never considered the man mad. Why she would be at his *domaine*, though... I have no answer to that.'

I tried to keep up with his list in my slow brain, but so far, what he'd said matched the information I'd already gathered. What if Cédric couldn't tell me anything new? Was I ready to give up?

'Five. Lucille Prunille, his mother. Lovely woman, very house-proud. One of those old-fashioned ones that had spent her life supporting her family but never setting up a career for herself. She entered the contest because it's what she'd done all her life, but not with any great hopes of winning.

'Six. Dina Amin. She was a new contestant that last time. She and her family had lived in the village for about three years and she wanted to have a go before they left. They already had plans to move north.'

Cédric stroked his beard. 'This is turning into quite a list. Seven. François.' He paused, seemingly weighing his words. 'I've come to know him better over the years.'

Was that a good thing or a bad thing? Where was he going with this?

'What you see is what you get with him. He's quick to rage, quick to forgive. Loves to be the centre of attention. So... I heard him threaten Louanne.'

Beau and I exchanged a look. Finally, some news!

'At the time, I thought she got what she deserved, and since I never took him seriously, I didn't tell the police. Now that I've known him for years, I've heard him threaten dozens of people, and it's never meant anything afterwards either, so I'll stick to my original judgement. However... of all the people on this list, he was the only one strapped for cash at the time.'

'Do you remember what he said?' Beau asked.

Cédric pressed his lips together and pulled the corners down. 'Something... something about getting what was owed or else she'd regret it. I can't remember exactly. It's only because you said it might have been for money instead of some personal motive that she was killed, that I thought of his threat again. Oh! I lied. He was not the only one in need of money.

'Eight. Margot Moulin, the judge. She was a piece of work. Flighty and air-headed most of the time, and then suddenly, she showed a shrewdness that bowled you over. But if you ask me, she was already on her way to the funny farm. I met someone once who knew her from years before, who said there was nothing ditzy about her then. That last competition, she'd just lost her business, and her mind wasn't sharp enough any more to set up another. So she could have been desperate for money too.'

He sat up and moved his hand through the air as if wiping something off a blackboard. 'Let me rephrase that. I know she needed money. I don't know how desperate she was.' Leaning back, he continued, 'Nine. Renate Reinhart. She was lovely and bubbly, full of hope for her career. Shame it never did take off. She knew nothing about cooking at all, but her agent had arranged this, so she made it work. I wonder if she would've done better with a different agent, but I believe they got married in the end, so...' He shrugged, leaving it there.

'And I suppose you'll want to add me as an even tenth. Because I was with the contestants that evening. The only sober one at that, since I was pouring. They'd had a day of sausage making, which is the most difficult bit, I've been told. So they got together to unwind at the *caveau*. Even Lucille Prunille had knocked back a few. Dina Amin walked her home earlier than the others, but Claudine, Louanne, and François were having a grand old time. That's when Louanne declared she knew all about what the village thought of her and what role Claudine and François had played in that, but it only seemed funny to them, the way they were laughing about it. Even after Louanne said she'd still win the next day.'

I narrowed my eyes. 'Auguste said he'd never seen Louanne drunk. Would you say she was?'

Stroking his beard, Cédric grinned. 'She was lathered. Gilles had to leave work early to take her home, poor man. I don't know how he did it, living with a shrew like that. Maybe you grow up meek if you're raised by your grandparents. But you know what they say – the meek shall inherit the earth. Don't think I'm in line for that.' He bellowed a laugh and got up. 'Now, if you don't mind, it's time for afternoon naps. I'll take her off you, Thibault.'

A princess transfer took place, after which Beau magically transformed his hair back to normal with two strokes of his hand. Why did he take so long in the morning if that was all he needed to do?

'Thank you, Cédric. That was very informative.'

He nodded, and with that, we were on our way back.

'So. She was sloshed. Does that make Gilles's accident theory more likely?' Beau asked.

I wasn't convinced. 'I'd say it's about 99 percent certain someone had a hand in her death. The only part of Gilles's theory that might make sense is the burglar caught in the act. Cédric summed it all up nicely for us, but he didn't add anyone new. The files Jacqueline sent me showed that the police interviewed almost everyone in the village at the time, but no one else seemed to have any kind of involvement with her. Other than seeing her at the *caveau*, it looks like most tried to stay well away.'

'So you think there's as much evidence for an unknown perpetrator as there is for anyone on the list?'

We'd taken a shortcut through Auguste's vineyards, but the path went uphill, and I stopped to catch my breath. Leaning on a wooden post at the end of one of the lines of vines, I pressed my hand to my side.

'Logically, I think we can exclude some of the people from that list, at least. Renate Reinhart, for instance.'

'All right, let's strike her off. Louanne was the victim and Auguste has a solid alibi, so that leaves seven.'

'How do you feel about Dina Amin?'

He stared out over the Saône valley. 'It's hard to say without actually being able to talk to them, but from what we know, I think we can exclude both Dina and Lucille. Nothing points to them having any kind of special negative relationship with Louanne, or a reason to want her so-called treasure.'

I nodded, resuming our walk. 'So that leaves five: Margot Moulin, Claudine Prunille, Gilles de Vigan, François Simon, and Cédric Roche.'

'With no evidence against any of them. Even if we discount Gilles and Cédric, we're still left with three suspects. We haven't done any better than the police thirty years ago.'

I gave him a sideways glance. 'Are you really surprised?'

He shrugged. 'Maybe I shouldn't be, but we've had such a good success rate lately... I thought this would be easy.'

I chuckled at his disheartened words. 'Let this be a lesson to you.'

'Right. Next murder, I won't think it'll be easy to solve.'

I cringed. 'Don't say that! Three murders is more than any twenty-two-year-old should have to deal with. Or any thirty-one-year-old.'

'Sooo... are we giving up?' There was a distinct reluctance in his voice.

If I were honest, giving up now would be extremely unsatisfying, but I had only one more question that might possibly be answered.

'What I want to know is why Louanne went to Auguste's at night after Gilles had already had to bring her home.' I sneeze-coughed, feeling my head grow heavy again.

Beau immediately perked up. 'Want to go and put the squeeze on Auguste? I missed out on the last interrogation, and our visit to Cédric didn't feel like one.'

Must have been the little princess on his lap.

'Hm. Him or Gilles. Gilles let her go out again, knowing she was drunk. But he couldn't have known where she'd go.'

'Auguste, then?'

I nodded and picked up the pace.

17
Much to learn

'You think the motive was greed?' The notion seemed to relieve Auguste for some reason. 'Ha! Well, that leaves us out of the equation then. We had nothing afterwards. No financial benefit for us.' He almost skipped through the kitchen to pull a handle from a cupboard.

Yves was standing at the ready at the meat grinder, but instead of meat, he held a bowl of chickpeas. 'I'm going to show *Papi* how delicious falafel can be,' he said, chucking a bunch of peas in the grinder bowl.

Handing him the handle, Auguste snorted. 'Apparently, we're not having any meat today. Not even chicken. The pup is going to cook for me.'

'This pup will show you the way.' Their bickering seemed to have evolved into good-natured banter, at least for the day. Yves, especially, was in an exceptionally good mood. He fixed the handle, but it would only turn in fits and starts. 'I think it needs a little love.' From the cupboard above, he pulled a little bottle of oil. 'Bottle o' love,' he declared, while oiling the machine. It didn't work.

Auguste laughed. 'I always left that thing to your grandmother.' Changing colour, he quickly added, 'It ran more smoothly then. So, greed? How did you work that out?'

'Véronique is looking for something valuable in the hotel,' Yves told the meat grinder before I had the chance to say anything. 'She's amazing. She showed me all this research she's done into what it could be that her mother left her.'

'Left her?' Beau asked. 'That sounds more like she knew she was going to die.'

'No, no.' He turned the handle another inch with a grunt. 'I'm probably not explaining it very well. Roni has noted down all the things she remembered her mother saying over the years and she's certain there was something valuable in the hotel. She made sure the renovations were postponed long enough for her to be here, so—'

'She what?' I felt my eyebrows knit together. Hearing Yves rave about Véronique's magnificence only confirmed how much Léon must love her, and I'd focussed on not pouting, but this revelation put her in a different light altogether. Suddenly, Léon's question about the date of the objections to our renovations made sense. He'd suspected it was Véronique who'd hindered our venture. She'd cost us thousands of euros! And Yves thought that was a clever move?

I opened my mouth to let him have it, but Beau saw it coming and intervened. 'Roni? You've seen more of each other, then?' While Yves elaborated on the genius that was Véronique, Beau pushed him gently out of the kitchen.

'We could have been well under way,' I seethed to Auguste at a much more civilised volume than I wanted to use.

He patted my shoulder with a sympathetic face. 'Yves has a lot to learn. A lot.' He looked me in the eye. 'As much as I like seeing you, Julie, I get the feeling you came here for a reason. What can I do for you?'

I smiled apologetically. 'The greed angle didn't get us anywhere, so we're more or less back to square one. Last time, I asked you if Louanne came here because she and Claudine were friends and you told me they weren't. So I still don't understand why she would come here.'

Auguste drew a quick breath through his nose and shuffled to the meat grinder to fiddle with it. 'I told you, we were... friends. She didn't know Claudine and I had switched. Ordinarily, I would have been here.'

'Without Claudine.' Looked like the rumours were true after all.

Auguste didn't turn to face me. *'Un verre de rouge?'*

Tempting, knowing the quality of Auguste's wine, but I shook my head, drawing a tissue from my purse instead. I withdrew to the corridor to blow my nose and heard Yves chatting to Thibault.

'First thing I'll do is plant two more cherry trees, so the name Domaine des Sept Cerisiers makes sense again. Roni thought that was a great idea.'

I bet she did. Cost other people money, that's what she did. Yves would have to print a whole new batch of labels because they now proudly showed five cherry trees instead of seven. It was a kind of running joke, according to Auguste. Much to learn, indeed.

I texted Jeanette about what I'd found out, but regretted the emotional message as soon as I'd sent it. I closed my eyes and put my finger and thumb to my temple, drawing out a particularly nasty string of thoughts. Negative ideas about myself were bad enough, but if I had them about others, my imaginary dirty rag turned even darker.

'Yves...' I said, gliding into the living room while flinging my brain filth further down the corridor. 'Last time, your grandfather mentioned that your grandmother couldn't stand Louanne, and you nodded. Did you know about their rivalry, or...?'

He laughed, in a carefree a way that convinced me he knew nothing of the affair. 'Nah! But *Mamie* was always very outspoken on that sort of thing. If she liked you, you couldn't do wrong. But if she didn't, you'd better run for cover.'

'I s—' I sneezed. 'Beau, I'd like to go back home now. You're welcome to stay, but...'

Beau rose. 'No, I'll come. Come round to ours some time,' he invited Yves.

Ours, was it? It still bugged me if he talked about my house like that. But since the brain fog had begun to rise again, I needed aspirin before I could berate him properly. We exited through the kitchen, where Auguste was attacking the ancient meat grinder with a screwdriver. Since it had been attached to the work surface for ages, it wouldn't budge. Auguste started when we said goodbye and hid the grinder from view as he held up his hand.

'Your Cactus may have a rival.' Thibault grinned as we trotted home.

'Don't call him... What do you mean?'

'If you're a smitten kitten, Yves is a... a...'

'Spellbound hound?' I offered, but Beau made a face.

'Let's stick to besotted fool.'

'Oh. Well, I like mine better. Thank you. I think.'

'Everything she's done is amazing and wonderful and fantastic.' He fluttered his eyelashes. 'But he refuses to admit he's in love with her.'

'He's only known her for a day.'

'Mneh.' He shrugged, as if falling in love was an everyday occurrence for him. But what did I know? Maybe it was.

It was getting dark when we reached my front door. Down the road, Anne-Bonny had all the lights in the house on. Her drive and part of the road were packed with cars, but, thankfully, no loud music. 'I think I'll make us some chicken soup.'

He grinned. 'You could use it. But it's hours before dinner. You hungry? I can get us a little *goûter* if I hurry. Might want some fresh bread with that soup.'

The French diet includes enough bread as it is, but with his friendship with the baker's daughter, I'd begun to feed half the bird population in the Beaujolais. 'Say hello to Céline for me.'

Yawning, I waved him goodbye, then had a coughing fit. That magical couch looked very appealing. Perhaps if I had another nap, I'd feel better again.

Unfortunately, sleep wouldn't come. I kept thinking about the mural at the hotel. With all the brouhaha surrounding Véronique and the mucus filling my head, I hadn't even given myself a minute to be happy for Jeanette and her new-found wealth. Who'd have thought that eyesore I couldn't wait to get rid of would bring her so much happiness?

A vision of Jessica Rose appeared. She'd saved it. But she'd done so at someone else's... request? Order? *Someone* knew it was there and that it was worth enough to save. But why hadn't they done so before? And why not come forward themselves?

Could it be that the mural was Louanne's valuable thing? No, that was impossible. The mural was put up after her death. Strange coincidence, though. Could there really still be something inside one of the lockers covered by the mural? Those conservation people had better hurry. But Jeanette would make sure of that, I had no doubt.

'Look who I found.' Beau barged in, followed by someone I only recognised as Léon when I'd put on my glasses.

My heart skipped a beat, I shot up, and my hand reached for my hair to redo my ponytail.

'No, don't get up. You need your rest. Maybe I shouldn't have come?' Léon cast Thibault a questioning look, as if Blondie would know what was best for me.

'Of course you should. I'm fine. Would you like some chicken soup?'

'Julie...' Beau sounded exasperated. 'It's not time for chicken soup yet. I'll get on that in a minute. Brought you an *hérisson*.'

He slid the plate with the nutty tartlet onto the coffee table, and I sat up straight. The little ganache spikes always made me smile.

'He said you liked them.' Beau offered this information from the kitchen, where I heard him rifle through the cutlery drawer.

I smiled at Léon. How could he remember those little things from years ago, while Beau still didn't know the dessert forks were kept in a different drawer? While I invited Léon to sit, Beau switched on the radio and started his usual humming along. He returned to the living room with another of his inventive lyrics.

'No dark Kardashians in the classroom,' he sang.

'Dark sarcasm!' Léon frowned in disbelief. 'Peasant.'

'Teacher,' I warned, 'leave the kid alone.'

He grinned, asking instead how I was feeling. With that out of the way, I couldn't help coming back to the investigations.

'Thibault and I went to see Cédric today.'

Léon's blank look told me he had no idea who I was talking about.

'He's an old friend of my mother's who was also involved with the *concours culinaire*.'

'Are you still...' He sighed. 'Anything?'

I rubbed my temple. 'We have the answer to all the *W* questions: who, what, where, when, how, and probably why. All we need to find out now is who by.'

'By whom,' Léon corrected.

'But then it doesn't start with *W*.' Sometimes I just want to be right.

'*How* doesn't start with *W*.' And Beau just had to be a smarty pants.

'Shut up,' I mumbled.

'But didn't you already know all the other things?'

In other words, like he and all the others had said before, this investigation wasn't going anywhere. None of the suspects seemed right, even after Cédric had listed them so neatly.

I lowered my gaze to the floor, a little deflated after I'd been so sure we were getting somewhere. Why did I have that feeling? What had I seen or heard that had convinced me I was going in the right direction? If only the cloud in my head would lift! I rubbed my temple again.

Still chewing on the last bite of his pastry, Beau declared, 'Léon and I are going to the *caveau* after dinner. Want to come?'

'Maybe she shouldn't—' Léon started.

'Yes.' I would take a whole packet of painkillers if it would let me spend more time with him. Okay, maybe that would not be a good idea as it might end my time. With anyone. But I would definitely take a painkiller now and join them in the *caveau* later.

Fortunately, aided by the little pill and my decision to let the investigation rest for the time being, my head cleared up while cooking and eating dinner. Léon helped me in the kitchen, so Beau got some well-deserved time off making my food. He used it to watch some spy show with a lot of gratuitous bra shots. Ordinarily, I would have made fun of him, but now, I was too busy enjoying the casual banter with the man who made my heart beat quicker. We talked about my business, his students, travel, foreign affairs, films, the weather, and the French Revolution, and we only stopped when Beau said he might not come along if we were going to be boring all night. Since by then we were already at the door to the *caveau*, we didn't take him seriously, but we both grinned like teenagers caught checking out the liquor cabinet and promised to behave.

Saint-Maurice's *caveau* was located in a cellar on the corner of the main road and the village square. To enter, you had to descend a few steps first outside and then more inside. At any other time than a Friday night, this passage would lead you to a series of vaulted rooms. Now it was packed with people and you could hardly get through the door. Standing on the top step, I saw my mother in the crowd and waved, but she hadn't noticed me. We threw ourselves in the throng to get from the first room, which contained only a few tables made of barrels and old photos and antique wine paraphernalia on the walls, to the second room, where the bar was.

'*Rouge ou blanc?*' Beau asked. The only thing served here was local wine. But since it was the only bar in the village, the small venue was doing very well indeed.

'Water,' I replied, and he nodded.

Léon found me a bar stool at one of the barrel tables, and I surveyed the crowd. From here, I couldn't see my mother, but everyone else seemed to be in attendance. François was holding court in the room running parallel to the entrance.

Throughout the week, this was where they'd set up a long table for people to meet. The council meetings, for instance, were sometimes held here. But on Friday and Saturday nights, that table took up too much space, and it was removed.

In François's audience I spotted Jeanette and Théo, as well as Yves. Cédric held a tray of glasses high above the crowd while he made his way from the bar to where I'd seen my mother. I liked coming here to people-watch, though at the moment, the din of everyone talking at once did nothing for my already buzzing head.

Cédric and François. Two of the people on my impossible list. I knew I shouldn't think about the investigation, but seeing them like that... Had one of them got away with murder? Thibault still suspected Margot, but there would be no way to prove it. Same went for Claudine. If he were right, we might as well give up our search. I had to remind myself that we e-ffectively had, but my eye was drawn to François again. Could I really give up if I wasn't absolutely sure I'd done every single thing I could think of?

Beau brought me my water, but he was distracted by a woman my mother's age, who was giving him a finger wave.

I pulled up my eyebrows, shouting over the noise. 'Aren't you a little—'

He stopped me with a held-up hand. 'I make it a point never to be out of anyone's league.'

I sipped my water to relieve my sore throat. 'I think you've succeeded.'

He grinned and gave a little wink. 'I'm a tramp, but you love me.'

'Ha!'

He spread his arms wide. 'What? I'm dashing and daring—'

'Courageous and caring? Because that would make you a Gummi Bear.' My mother's eyes twinkled over the rim of her wine glass.

He gave her a puzzled look, and she sighed.

'I hate when people are too young to understand my jokes.'

'I know the Gummi Bears,' Léon offered, while Beau slipped away.

'I like you already. I'm Flora. Didn't I see you this morning at the hotel? What a commotion that was.'

From her chattiness I deduced that my mother had been here a while. This was certainly not her first glass.

'You must be Julie's mother. Léon Levotre.' Look at that smile! How could my mother do anything but swoon? Instead, she looked surprised, though in a pleasant kind of way.

'I see! You're the person I have to thank for saving my daughter's sanity.'

'*Maman...*' I groaned.

For some reason, Léon and my mother held a staring match, which she gave up after a few awkwardly long seconds. 'I hope we'll see more of you, Monsieur Levotre.'

You and me both, *Maman.*

'Thank you. Please call me Léon.'

I spent about a glass and a half lazily and contentedly listening to my mother and my friend getting to know each other, while the chatter around us gradually got more and more animated as people consumed more of the local speciality.

Cédric came up behind Léon and clapped him on the shoulder. 'Nice to meet you, Léon,' he said after introductions had been made. 'I'm Cédric. That pretty lady over there with the orange hair is my wife. Don't bother trying to pronounce her name. She's foreign.' He smiled and waved at a woman at the other end of the bar, who blew him a kiss. 'Still on the lookout for greed, Juju? Where's *le petit prince?*'

I looked in the direction of the woman who'd leered at Thibault earlier, but she was alone. She must not have 'needed' him. I shrugged. 'He's around.'

My mother's gaze flicked between Cédric and me. 'What greed?' As the mayor of a small village, she considered it her duty to know everything that went on around here. Meaning that if it looked like she'd missed something, especially something concerning her family, she would fight a dragon to find out about it.

'Maybe Louanne was killed because of the valuable thing Véronique says she hid?'

The change in my mother was remarkable. All curiosity left her eyes, and she stared at me with a mixture of concern and mild panic. Her gaze shot to François, who happened to look her way at the same moment. His eyebrows drew together as well, and with a silencing gesture to the person he'd been speaking to, he came our way.

'Something wrong, Flora?'

Maman shook her head, but her voice wavered when she said, 'N-no, no. There's nothing.'

'Is this about Louanne again?' He turned towards Léon and me. 'I told you before, the only thing you'll achieve is to upset people. You won't find anything new.'

'Not even if the motive is greed?' Léon said.

His unexpected words had me narrow my eyes. I thought he wanted me to stop looking? Then why was he trying to aggravate François? And why was he succeeding?

18

Very satisfying

François lost all colour except for the red veins on his nose. Even the tipsy blush on his cheeks disappeared. His gaze snapped to Cédric. 'Do they... I mean, how have they... You were in much deeper than me. You should—'

'I can't believe she'd disrupt our plans like that.' Jeanette came up on my other side and made me jump. 'Who does she think she is, costing us thousands of euros because of some hunch?'

Desperate to get back to eavesdropping on the conversation happening on my other side, I tried to appease my friend. 'I know. And the fact that they listened to her!' My voice was breaking, and I took another sip of water. 'I should ask her what arguments she used. But look at it this way – if she hadn't stopped us, we'd never have found out about the value of the ugly mural, and you wou—'

'Isn't that her?'

My head snapped towards the entrance. Véronique had indeed come in, wearing a sparkly red dress that poked my green-eyed monster into raging action. It showed off her willowy figure to perfection, and here I was, snotty-nosed, nursing a headache, and bespectacled, to top it all off. From the corner of my eye, I saw that Léon had noticed her too. How could he not? She made quite an entrance. Even Cédric and François had stopped talking to see what I was glowering at.

'Hey!' Jeanette called out to someone bumping into her. He turned unsteadily to apologise but flinched when he recognised me, his dramatic blue eyes widening.

And then I remembered what I'd seen and heard. The elusive bit of information that had made me determined not to give up my search, even though I couldn't remember what it was. Now I knew.

'Yves! That meat grinder—'

He gulped in air as he backed away. 'No! He didn't mean it that way. He said... It's not...'

Without explanation, he turned and jumped towards the exit, but both François and Cédric were in the way.

'*Ouh lá,*' Cédric said, but François, whose colour had risen along with his temper, fuelled by the alcohol in his blood, grabbed the young man by the collar.

'If you don't apologise this instant,' he growled, 'I'll—'

Yves tore himself free and stumbled backwards. He turned to run, but this time it was Thibault who was in his way. If only he'd mumbled an apology, that would have been the end of it, but with tension mounting, he shoved Beau's shoulder.

Before anyone knew what had happened, Yves was sprawled backwards on the floor, staring up at an angry Beau. My jaw dropped. I'd never known my puppy of an assistant to be so aggressive. What was going on?

The entire bar had stilled, not used to anything other than friendly discussions on a Friday night.

François was at Beau's side in an instant, forming a front against Yves. 'You see what happens to disrespectful people?'

Behind me, I heard the barman push himself around the counter, but Léon had already offered his hand to Yves. Yves used it to pull himself to standing, but then shoved Léon backwards into François while he tried to make his way to the exit.

Cédric, wine in hand, mumbled an 'Eh, not fair', but it was Beau again who flew at Yves. Two elderly ladies saw the bundle of limbs coming towards them and jumped aside. Beau's momentum threw Yves off course, and they slammed into one of the barrel tables. Glasses and bottles crashed to the floor. A few men in suits jumped out of the way of the splattering wine, but with everyone pushing forwards to see the fight, a domino effect had people behind the suits bumping into other tables, knocking over more wine.

Some of the people further back, who couldn't see what was going on, started pushing against the flow, launching those at the front into the line of fire. A woman caught the edge of Yves's fist that was meant for Thibault, and her husband took a menacing step forward. He grabbed one of the wine bottles and swung at Yves, who was too busy dodging Beau to notice. The bottle flew from the man's hand and hit Charles Cochon, the butcher, in the arm. Charles drew himself up and glared at the man, who cowered and turned to care for his wife.

Yves dodged the wrong fist and went down when Beau punched him full on the mouth. Véronique screamed. Cédric, still casually holding his wine, winced at the sound so close to his ear and said something to her that earned him an open-mouthed scowl.

All this happened in a matter of seconds. I caught sight of my mother, who was clearly debating whether it was wise to start mayoring, but when Charles Cochon charged at the bottle-slinger with a barstool, she couldn't very well stand aside and do nothing. With a whoop, she threw herself in front of Charles, waving her arms and making herself as big as possible, reaching just about to Charles's midriff. Physically, she might not mean much, but she can death-stare with the best of them. Charles knew what was good for him and lowered the barstool.

François, who had been charging at Yves the moment he went down, now barrelled into the caring husband, and the two of them tumbled to the floor, becoming instantly soaked with Beaujolais wine. Léon worked his way forward to pick them both up but took a punch to the arm. He staggered sideways into a table, grabbed one of the fallen bottles, and weighed it in his hand, casting calculating glances at it and Beau's skull.

Enough was enough. Not particularly trusting Léon's aim nor the effect a hit would have on either of them, I hopped off my barstool. Unfortunately, that meant my eyes were now lower, and I couldn't see over Cédric's shoulder. I climbed back on, tucking my knees under me, and put my hands to my mouth. I yelled at the top of my lungs, but no sound came out. Not even a rasp. Since I'd lost my voice anyway, I cursed out loud.

Beau staggered backwards, clutching his stomach after Yves had planted his foot there. He caught sight of Léon with the bottle and frowned, but then pointed at Yves, who was clambering to his feet, and shouted, 'Cactus, watch out!'

New plan. I took off my stiletto heel, ready to launch myself into battle. I would whack their heads in. I would bring order. I would... I looked at my makeshift weapon. If I wielded that, I would actually whack their heads in.

New plan number two. I brought that heel down on the table in front of me as hard as I could. It rang out like a gunshot. The silence in the bar was instant. Many of the patrons held their arms over their heads. I waved my arms to grab people's attention, but couldn't say a thing.

A hollow thump was the only answer to my attempts, followed by my mother's voice. 'All right, that's enough. Anyone still bearing a grudge can come to me, and we'll work something out. Otherwise, go get cleaned up or enjoy your drinks in peace.'

A new hubbub started, this time the more subdued buzz of people collecting their things and leaving. I spotted Céline in the crowd, looking distressed. I'd have to remember to send her a soothing message after I'd spoken to the one probably responsible for her discomfort. The bar personnel started rapidly cleaning up, throwing us accusing looks, but not daring to say anything in front of the boss's daughter. Soon, the only ones left were my friends. And Véronique. She sat on the floor next to Yves and cooed in his ear. Yves sported bruises and cuts all over his face, but it was his general air of defeat that made me feel for him.

Beau stared at Léon. 'Did you just clonk Yves on the head with a wine bottle?'

'That was *you*?' Yves threw Léon a vicious look, adjusting the ice pack on the back of his head.

'Yes, very satisfying. But honestly, it seemed less painful than what you were doing to him. I mean, what was that all about?'

Beau actually turned pink. I agreed with Léon. This was very satisfying indeed.

'You don't grow up in my family without learning how to fight.'

'That was not a fight. That was carnage.'

Thibault glanced at Yves and winced. 'I, err… I'm sorry, *frérot*.'

Yves gave a half-shrug. 'I shouldn't have shoved you.'

'No, but… really… I went too far.'

'Yes, yes, you're both sorry. Get over it' is what I wanted to say. What came out was a high-pitched wheeze that made everybody, including Yves, pity me instead. I threw both my hands up, then dug into my purse for my phone. I tapped a message, then gave the phone to Yves.

He read what I'd written and frowned. 'Really? But *Papi* thinks…'

I bobbed my head left and right, holding up my palms.

Véronique grabbed my phone off Yves and read my message out loud. '*I don't think she did it.* Who did what?'

'My grandmother,' Yves said to the floor tiles. 'I thought she might have killed your mother.'

With a gasp, Véronique blanched, pressing her fingers to her lips.

Yves looked back up at me. 'After you left, *Papi* took the meat grinder off the kitchen counter. He said it could be evidence. I didn't understand, but he said you figured it out.'

He'd given me too much credit. I only worked out just now that if Claudine was strong enough to work that meat grinder, she might have been strong enough to handle a struggling Louanne. But even then, a meat grinder is a very different thing from a woman fighting for her life. Even a drunk one.

Still, Auguste must have suspected his wife all these years. That's why he was so happy to hear I was looking into greed as a motive. But though he probably had good reason to suspect Claudine, I trusted my mother's judgement of the situation at the time. Without any more evidence than some old meat grinder, I wasn't going to accuse a woman who was no longer around to defend herself.

'Your grandmother killed my mother?' Véronique's whispered words were meant only for Yves.

He shrugged. 'My grandfather said she always denied it, but why else would your mother have died in our home?'

'But there is still no evidence one way or another, is there?' Léon asked.

I shook my head.

'I don't believe it,' Cédric stated.

François shook his head. 'Me neither.'

Maman smiled. 'Nope.'

Véronique only placed her hand on Yves's.

We all went our separate ways when the bar personnel said they were closing up, but Léon held me and Beau back.

'Can you stop now?' he pleaded with me.

I swallowed and nodded, keeping my head bent. He'd asked me before, but my stubbornness had got Yves beat up. By Beau no less. Léon couldn't have seen that coming, but he'd probably been right in the first place.

Beau put his arm around my shoulders and steered me home. 'He's not really mad at you,' he said after we'd gone halfway in silence.

I huffed.

'Even if he is, he won't be forever.'

I didn't answer. For one, my voice didn't work, but for two... I wasn't so sure I hadn't really messed it up this time. Léon's disappointment in me was a lot harder to bear than if he had been angry.

Suddenly, Beau laughed. 'He clobbered Yves *after* you shot your shoe. "Very satisfying".' His impression of Léon was on point, as usual. 'Looks like he's not such a cold fish about having a rival after all.'

I hung my head a little lower, and Beau rubbed my arms. 'Aww. You'll get over it.'

'Thanks,' I croaked, turning the key in my front door. Did he really think I was going to take life lessons from a twenty-two-year-old?

He chuckled, but gave me a bear hug from behind, which at least made me smile. 'Oh, I should message Céline. She looked very upset.'

Only one in two of my words came out audible, but Beau turned pink again. Rubbing his neck, he stared at the hallway floor. 'I... should call her.' He took a breath. 'We were talking. Céline and Yves and I. But he was drunk and... he didn't mean it like that. He was raving about Véronique, but he compared her to Céline, kind of... listing all the ways in which Véronique was better, you know? He didn't realise how he was making her feel, but I... got a bit mad.'

I gave him a stern look, then shook my head and turned, not wanting to use my voice any more than I had to. Drifting into the kitchen, I dumped my purse on the table, when something glinting caught my eye. I picked it up and gasped.

'What?' Beau hurried to my side, ready to catch me or put out a fire, but when he saw what I was holding, he recoiled. 'Where did you get that?'

I stared at my father's signet ring. The one I'd given to Franck when we first got together. The one he'd worn with such superiority and rubbed in my face every time he forced me to do something. I pointed at the kitchen table.

'How did it get there?'

'Maybe... Léon?' I whispered. That must be it. Léon was the only one who'd been in today. I'd have to ask him how he got hold of it.

Thibault's eyes were dark. Thinking of Franck always did that, but I got the feeling Beau didn't believe the ring came from Léon. But how else would it have got here? Franck was still in prison. He couldn't get to me.

I repeated that to myself all the way to my bed, trying to suppress the niggling doubt. I thought about sending Léon a message but kept seeing the disappointment in his face. I'd talk to him tomorrow and ask him then.

19
No

Three Decades earlier

Flora spent the next few hours after the conversation with François at home, watching TV and feeling miserable. Not even her new Disney movie could take her mind off things. She kept remembering Nico's disgusted expression. Halfway through the latest episode of MacGyver, she couldn't take it any more. She switched off the TV and pulled her knees up to her chin. Would François have met with Louanne in her stead? And what was up with Isabelle and her odd behaviour around Louanne? Was she involved too? But how? François never mentioned her. Maybe Flora should have gone to the meeting and confronted them.

But an hour ago, she was still crying over losing Nicolas. It was supposed to be *her* decision to leave *him*, not the other way round. And certainly not this way. He was going to despise her forever, for something she didn't even do. Or maybe *because* she didn't do anything. Now, she cried again because if she hadn't cried an hour ago, she might have saved her marriage.

The marriage she hadn't been sure she wanted until it was too late.

Had Nicolas been right after all? Had she just needed some more time to get used to the idea? Oh, what was the point thinking about that, anyway? He'd already given up on her. And with good reason. Someone had told her the village was under attack from the sneakiest of killers, and what was she doing? Crying over being such a… *lavette*.

Flora sat up straight and took a deep, faltering breath. Dishcloth no more. If she were to live her life without her love, she might as well try to save the village before moving away from it. Forever. She wiped her eyes with the back of her hand and reused a tissue that still seemed okay to blow her nose in.

First things first. She needed a plan. A good plan. A solid plan. She needed to not simply walk out the door and hope for the best. Except that's exactly what she was doing. Though even twilight was on its last legs, she donned her biggest pair of sunglasses. It wasn't much of a disguise, but it felt like a shield between her and whatever else the outside world was going to throw at her today. Now for that plan…

Though Cogny was a village of less than 850 people, it had been growing more rapidly recently, leading to the construction of the block of flats in La Brosse where Nicolas lived. But La Brosse was up the hill, on the other side of the village from where Flora lived. In the whole ten minutes it took to get from here to there, she should have plenty of time to come up with some sort of plan.

Crossing the Place de l'Église with its wooden stage now abandoned, she passed Apolline and her friend, who were giggling on a bench, working their way through heaps of gelato.

'I know! He's dreamy,' Apolline told her friend. 'And you know he'll be, like, the next mayor or something. If I had him, I'd never let him go. Status is everything, my friend.'

Flora had been about to start weeping again until that statement. Jealousy stabbed her in the gut. Apolline had no right to be talking about her and Nicolas like that! Then guilt crept up on her. Apolline couldn't be talking about Nicolas. He didn't care about status. He cared about this village. Her village. The one she was about to save. If she could come up with a plan.

Somehow, she'd ended up in front of Nicolas's flat, but she still didn't have a plan. There was no other way. She'd simply have to tell Nicolas everything that had happened and hope that his brain would work better than hers. He'd probably been wise enough to eat dinner...

The door opened half a second after her knock, as if he'd been waiting for her. But it wasn't Nicolas who opened it. It was Cédric. And François was also there, waiting for Nicolas to hang up the phone. Dragging herself inside, Flora joined the others in silent expectation, while Nicolas slowly hung up and turned.

'She's dead.'

Jaws dropped, then all eyes cut to Flora. *I'm not dead*, was her first thought. 'Who?'

'Louanne,' Nicolas explained. 'They found her at Auguste's, drowned in the open press.'

The three others winced, but Flora still felt their eyes on her. Then she realised what they must all be thinking. 'No!' she shouted at Nicolas, eyes wide.

Nicolas frowned. 'No?'

'I didn't kill her!'

The perplexity on his face was absolute. 'Of course not! I thought you meant, no, you didn't want to marry me.'

The change of subject was ridiculous but drove all other thoughts from Flora's mind. 'You still want to marry me?'

'Of course!'

Flora's knees buckled, and Cédric rushed to catch her, while Nicolas pulled out a chair for her and knelt beside her after she'd sat down. So many thoughts and feelings hurtled over each other in her mind that she couldn't focus on any. Instead, she reverted to the one thought that had driven her here. 'But I have no plan.'

Nicolas didn't understand. 'We don't have to get married straight away. There's plenty of time for a plan. Right now, I think we need to revisit another plan.' He looked the other two in the eyes.

'That's what I—' *Oh, who cares.* He still wanted to marry her. As soon as that settled as the new base of her existence, she could finally give her attention to the disturbing news Nicolas had received. She listened to the barrage of questions the other men now fired at Nicolas, who hadn't heard any more than that Louanne had been found dead in Auguste's wine press.

'Is it murder?'

'They don't know yet.'

Only then did it really hit Flora that Louanne was dead. She gasped, pressing her fingers to her mouth. 'I was supposed to be there. If I'd been with her, she might still have been alive.'

François shook his head. 'No, she always leaves the crates out. They'll probably still be there.'

Nicolas looked up, but it was Flora who said, 'Then we can intercept them. Make sure they don't end up in the wrong hands.'

'On my way.' Cédric was halfway out the door when he said it. François followed at a gallop.

Nicolas, still on his knees beside her, rubbed Flora's legs.

'I'm sorry,' she whispered.

'For what?'

'For making you so angry with me.'

'How many times do I have to say this? I wasn't angry. I will wait.'

'No, at François's car. You ran off.'

He looked puzzled for a moment, then laughed. Laughed! 'I wasn't angry with you! I'd never seen you like that. I had to take a moment not to beat up François for making *you* so angry!'

All she could do was stare at him.

Still grinning, Nicolas continued, 'But I turned back and you were already gone. That's when he confessed to all that had happened and what he and Cédric suspect. We picked up Cédric from the hotel and have been trying to come up with a plan to catch Louanne in the act, so to speak.'

To save the village. He didn't need her at all. 'And now she's dead.'

'Yes...'

'Do you think the drugs people killed her?'

Nicolas shrugged. Neither of them knew what to say or do.

'I couldn't think of a plan.' For some reason, it was important that he knew how useless she was. If he still wanted her, he should know all about that.

Nicolas straightened and pulled her up as well, leading her to the couch. 'All right, tell me about this all-important plan.'

'It's about Louanne.'

'Oh?' His sudden frown told Flora he'd not expected that.

'I tried to work out how I could stop her, but my brain is useless.'

He stroked her cheek with a crooked smile. 'No, it's not. If it's any consolation, the three of us had made and rejected about ten plans before that phone call. Now none of them are any good.'

'You're not giving up on me?'

He kissed her tenderly. 'I'll never give you up.'

'And I'll never let you down.'

He grinned, announcing a bad joke. 'I'll never turn around and des—'

'No.'

'No?' His eyebrows shot up, but he was going to have to get used to that word. Ever since she'd said it to François, it had settled in her mind and taken root. No was a pretty good word, actually. Small but powerful. Like she would be. With Nicolas by her side, she could handle everything village life would throw at her.

'I'm not going to travel the world with you. But I will marry you.'

20

You thought I was prickly?

'When we recovered the bottles, they contained nothing but wine. Bad wine, but still. We had absolutely no proof that anything drug-related had ever taken place. The police were suspicious of François at first, thinking he might have killed the competition, but he'd been with Cédric and *Papa* all night.'

Maman had that dreamy look in her eye she always got when talking about *Papa*. She'd come round to see how I was after losing my voice the night before. Since I actually felt a lot better, I'd offered her coffee, and now that I'd told her I wasn't going to dig any deeper, she'd got loose-lipped about the moment in her life that should have been amazing but would forever be overshadowed by the event that followed. 'So you see, it was because of the murder that we got married.' She sipped her coffee, lost in satisfied thoughts about Dad for a moment. During the course of her story, we'd worked our way through my tin of cookies, and she took the last one.

'I'd say that's a bit of a stretch.' I grinned. I'd heard the story of Dad's proposal before but never in this light. It was eye-opening. If only she'd told me before, then I could have ruled out both François and Cédric from the beginning.

'*Papa* kept an eye on those two from then on, and in return for his silence, they sometimes did him favours. All within the boundaries of the law, of course. Aunt Géraldine was right about your dad being a bit of a privateer. A free spirit in a suit jacket, that's how I always saw him. David inherited the suit jacket part, and you're the next free spirit.' She stroked my hair like she'd done when I was little and again when she'd found me in Villefranche. 'I'm so thankful that man hasn't broken you. But you need to take better care of yourself. Trouble seems to find you everywhere you go, and now you're sick.'

'Thank you for coming, *Maman*, but it really is just a cold. My voice is back, and I have an errand to run, so I'll see you later, okay?'

My mother drained her coffee cup and let herself be swept out the door. We saw enough of each other not to be offended by abrupt behaviour. And hearing her talk had switched on a light in my brain that had finally cleared the fog. There was someone I needed to speak to.

Hand on the door-knob, I thought about taking Beau with me, but it was a Saturday. He wouldn't be up for at least another hour. I closed the door behind me and took the road towards downhill, away from the village. Now that my brain was working again, I replayed all the conversations I'd had in the last few days, and this explanation of Louanne's murder – and I did think it was murder – was the only thing that fit. Still, it seemed outlandish. How would they react when I told them my findings?

'Julie? Come in. What an unexpected pleasure. I heard about last night. Are you feeling better?' Gilles looked both ways down the street before closing the door behind me. 'Véronique is still asleep, I'm afraid. She stayed with the neighbours until late, but she told me Yves felt much better by the time she left.'

I wasn't sure how Léon would feel about her spending that much time with Yves. But I had to try and see the good in Véronique if I were to remain friends with Léon. Apart from her greedy streak, she'd been friendly to me. At first. I still didn't like that she'd cost us a lot of money, but in the end, she'd made us more by giving us time to discover the Luc Leduc mural. And with the care she'd given Yves, I could see why Léon had fallen for her. I sighed. Telling her I was not going to continue my investigation was going to be hard. But sometimes, saying no is all you can do.

Gilles led me into a light and airy living room. The few pieces of furniture all had clean lines and were probably quite expensive, despite their deceptively simple forms. Abstract art adorned the walls and several pedestals around the room, which was the complete opposite of Auguste's old-fashioned, cosy, but dark house.

Gilles waved me into a chair by the fire and sat down opposite, dragging a hand through his thick, white hair, a curious look in his eyes. 'So, you don't think it was Claudine? Well, maybe it was a burglar after all.'

'I don't think so, Gilles. Véronique was right, *tu vois*. There was something valuable in the hotel.'

'Ah, yes, that painting. Who made that, again?'

'Luc Leduc.'

Gilles jutted out his lower lip. 'Never heard of him.'

'He was a relatively unknown local artist thirty years ago, but he's gained international renown since. Unlike' – I pointed at the sculpture to my right – 'his friend and colleague, Esmeralda Quimper.'

Pressing his lips together, Gilles narrowed his eyes. 'I didn't know you were interested in modern art,' he said quietly.

'It's actually my mother who's more of an art expert. I knew you'd replaced the traditional grapey decor in the *caveau* with modernist paintings, but I didn't make the connection until this morning. You were the one who alerted Jessica Rose.'

Gilles nodded slowly, leaning back and steepling his fingers in front of him.

'So why wait thirty years, if you knew it was there?'

'I'm a patient man, Julie,' he said quietly. 'I wouldn't have married Louanne if I weren't. I take my time to think things over. That painting wasn't worth much when the hotel closed. I knew it was going up in value, but the owners had sold to the council, and frankly, I didn't want them owning it. Also, I'm afraid I'm a tad – okay, maybe very – spiteful. I resented the fact that I hadn't bought any work by him when he was the local arrogant artist. But in the end, I couldn't let you destroy it. I've always supported local business owners. Even when they wreck my place...'

He gave me a dark look, and I felt heat creeping up my cheeks.

'So I hope you'll do some good for the community with it.'

'Jeanette will.' I nodded fervently in hopes of shaking off my deep blush. 'She had no part in the fight yesterday.'

Gilles gave a smile that didn't reach his eyes. 'So now you know.'

'Yes,' I said, looking him square in the eyes. 'I know. As much as you love it, the *caveau* wasn't yours, was it? You inherited it, but not from your parents.'

Breaking eye contact, Gilles stood up and moved to stand by the fire, his hand resting on the mantle. 'Go on.'

'It was Louanne's, but she never appreciated its value to the community. She only saw its monetary worth. What was her dream, Gilles? A similar place, but in the city?'

He huffed a dry laugh. 'Her dreams included only her. No community, not even a family. She was going to give away the *caveau* to win the contest. With no particular talent and only the few prizes in a local cooking contest, she thought she was going to make it big. She told me that night, she was going to leave Roni and me behind with nothing. My "precious community" would find me a "real" job.'

Sighing, he stared into the fire. 'Patience can only stretch so far, you know.' He picked up the poker and turned.

My eyes widened. I'd only come here to ask for the truth. Not for one second had I thought that kind old Gilles would not appreciate my candour. How naive! I knew he'd killed before, and I hadn't even bothered to wake Thibault. I gripped the armrests of my chair, ready to bolt.

'Have you told anyone?'

Panic rose. 'Yes! My friend Jacqueline with the police knows. She's on her way.'

Gilles blinked in confusion, then looked at the poker in his hand and laughed. 'No, you haven't. Silly girl.' He turned back to the fire and poked it with the iron rod.

Was he playing with me? I glanced at the door, judging whether I'd make it out before he could reach me, but then Gilles returned the poker to its stand and sat back down.

I let out a long breath. Good, I could still judge a character. It took a minute for my heart rate to go down, though.

Gilles planted his elbows on his knees and rubbed his forehead. 'When I came home, covered in grape juice, I was sure the police would know instantly that I was the murderer. Someone would have seen me, or they could tell from the way I'd held her under in an embrace that it must have been me. I even tripped over those stupid bottles of imported wine for Isabelle. Made an almighty racket that I was sure would have given me away. I thought about giving myself up. But they never found any evidence. Nobody really seemed to care. I felt a little guilty about that judge, but she shouldn't have played into Louanne's hand.'

Imported wine! Isabelle was involved after all, but for a shameful rather than an illegal affair. I felt only a little guilty for my feeling of triumph that I now held this piece of information that would surely come in handy one day. But now was not the time to gloat. 'For the last thirty years, Auguste has thought that his wife killed yours.'

Gilles snapped up straight, a cold glee in his eyes. 'Serves him right! Then he shouldn't have kissed my wife. I saw them! If things had gone to plan, he would have been convicted of her murder.' His shoulders sagged. 'But I'm glad he wasn't. It seemed the perfect revenge in the moment, but with time, perspectives change.' He looked at me, a sad but resigned look. 'So. What are you going to do?'

I stared at him. He wanted *me* to do something? 'There is no more evidence now than there was thirty years ago.'

He frowned. 'But *you* know.'

I held up my palms. 'That's not evidence. We're not going to find anything in the lockers, are we?'

'No, of course not. I took back the deed to the *caveau* the next day.'

'Well then. Unless you want to give yourself up...'

'You won't tell?'

'No. You could easily deny it. And I promised my friend I would stop digging.' I'd thought about telling Jacqueline, of course. With my mother's new information had come the realisation that it could really only have been Gilles who had motive, means, and opportunity. But what good would it do? In thirty years, Gilles hadn't murdered anyone else, as far as I could tell. He'd been a model citizen, doing good for the community left and right. I still felt he should pay for his actions, but unless he confessed, I had nothing that could put him away.

Gilles considered me for a few long seconds, then leaned back in his chair. 'Were you really scared of me just now?'

It came out with such amusement that I had to lie. 'I knew I was never in any real danger.'

He simply smiled.

I stayed a little longer, chatting about this and that, mostly how scared he'd been for Véronique's future if he had been found out. I made one last appeal to his better nature, which I felt was the least I had to do in the name of justice. I could tell on him, but officially, nothing would change. Unofficially, nobody cared any more. That much had become clear from my conversations around the village. It came down to him whether he'd tell his daughter or anyone else involved.

I'd just settled on the couch with my book and a cup of coffee when I had to get up again to answer the door. My stomach did that squeezy thing it always did when I saw Léon. But now it squeezed extra hard, knowing I'd upset him yesterday.

'I can't stay long,' he said as he entered the kitchen and sat on one of the chairs.

I poured him a coffee. 'Véronique waiting?'

His eyebrows raised. 'No, we broke up. I'm surprised you didn't notice.'

My heart did a hop, a skip, and a beat before I could feign mild interest. 'Oh? Why?'

One of those amazing smiles came my way, enchanting me into staring at his face. 'Seeing you again, I realised I wasn't in love with her. Hadn't been for a while.'

I gasped. He couldn't mean what I thought he meant? Had he even said what I thought he said?

Léon took my stunned silence the wrong way, and his smile faltered. 'So… Thibault called me Cactus yesterday. I imagine that is not something he invented?'

My heart dropped to my heels. Hadn't I told Beau not to call Léon that? Now I had to confess. 'No… That was what I saved you as in my phone. I never thought to change it.'

'You thought I was prickly?'

'No!' He must know that wasn't it. But this was the real confession I dreaded, though maybe not as much after what he'd said. Heat stung my cheeks as I stammered, 'I was married. Not happily, but still tied. It was a reminder… not to… get too close.'

He held my gaze, first with a smile, then with a building intensity that had my breath go so shallow, I was getting light-headed.

Suddenly, he broke eye contact and I felt as though I'd been dropped from an airplane. 'I'd better get to the airport.'

Wait, what? That wasn't supposed to happen! 'Whuh…' was all I managed.

'Didn't I tell you? I have a new job lined up in America. I wanted to help Véronique before I went back.'

Again, he seemed oblivious to the world crumbling around us. That was it? He was just going to leave? Like that?

At the front door, he turned and looked me in the eye. 'You've done enough, you know. You've already been accepted in the village. That moment has come and it has passed. You don't have to try so hard any more.'

Though it wasn't what I wanted him to say, tears stung behind my eyes. My head was swimming with fifteen things I wanted to say, all vying for first in line. I tried to form words, but for some reason, my voice had given up again. All that came out was, 'Okay.'

'It's... only for a few months. I'll be back by summer.' He hesitated, playing with the door handle as though he wanted to say more. 'Would you... like to stay in touch, or is that... too close?'

I nodded and shook my head at the same time. 'Yes. No! Yes, I want to stay in touch – no, I wouldn't mind if you got too close. At all. Really.'

He pulled up one corner of his mouth, the twinkle back in his eyes, and opened the door. 'I have to go.'

I stood a little straighter, still not sure if I should show the sunshine that was coming from within.

Léon's lips twitched. 'I'll miss the sexy way you shake your hair out before you put it in a ponytail.'

He thought I was sexy! The bright heat inside crept up my neck and came out through my cheeks, my eyes, and the biggest smile I'd ever smiled.

'There's really only one more thing...'

Huh? Oh right, the ring. I wanted to thank him for returning it, but Léon stepped closer and cupped my face with his hands. Those beautiful eyes closed, and I held my breath.

His kiss was all a kiss should be. Soft. Tender. Promising. And way too short. I held on to his lapels, yearning for more, but he only chuckled softly.

'I have to go or I'll miss my plane. But I will be back. Soon. Very soon.'

He kissed me again. A little less soft and a little more promising that time, but he still broke it off and left me leaning against the door frame, waving at his departing car. How had I gone from dread to hope to despair to elation to sadness and loss in the space of under five minutes?

The car had been gone for some time when I finally closed the door. Thibault was at the end of the corridor, sipping coffee.

'Were you spying on us?'

He shrugged. 'Not really. I was in full view. You just didn't see me.'

I walked past him into the living room to pick up my own cold coffee.

'You're unnaturally quiet,' he declared, helpfully.

I didn't answer.

'So that's the man of your dreams, huh?'

Ten years ago, I wouldn't have believed it, but yes, he so was. And now he was gone. Again. I looked at Beau, not knowing how to explain.

He looked back at me, strangely seeming to know exactly what I meant, but not knowing what to do.

'I could use a hug.' Contrary to what they say, people often like to be told what to do. You just have to know how to formulate the instructions.

Smiling, he stepped in and wrapped his arms around me. I sighed, trying to let go of this impractical blue feeling. Thibault was still holding me. He was no Léon, but he was nice and warm. Sometimes, Blondie knew exactly what was best for me.

'Oh! I forgot to thank him for the ring.'

Thibault let go of me, hiding his face in his mug. He didn't want to say it, but he was worried about something. I wondered if it had something to do with his so-called family emergency. I'd talk to him about that later, but for now, I had something else to ask.

'Do *you* think I've been accepted by the village?'

He plopped down on a chair. 'From the very beginning. Also, I think this whole thing has shown that even people who are very much rooted in the community aren't always the best ones. Small community can make for small minds. Sometimes you're better off with someone from the outside.'

Look at young Beau playing the philosopher. I knew he meant me, but I thought of another outsider. One with the best kisses. I couldn't wait for summer.

Other books by Christa Bakker

Acknowledgements

My heartfelt thanks to Kristen Tate at The Blue Garret for yet again taking my story and making it into something book-worthy. You are an outstanding editor!

Thanks also to Ailsa Body, Carole Marples, and Willy de Zoete for reading an unedited draft and giving lots of great advice on how to improve. Hugs all around!

A very grateful apology to Nienke Grasset for rushing her to have a look at my French during a very busy time. Amazing lady!

My wonderful husband and children deserve credit for letting me stare into the middle distance working out plot points when I should be paying attention to them. Unfortunately, there's another book coming...

Editing by Kristen Tate at The Blue Garret

Book cover by Christa and Erik Bakker

1st edition 2023

Visit the author's website at: www.christabakker.com